All on the Irish Shore

E. Somerville and Martin Ross

Contents

ALL ON THE IRISH SHORE

BY

E. Somerville and Martin Ross

THE TINKER'S DOG

Can't you head 'em off, Patsey? Run, you fool! *run*, can't you?"
Sounds followed that suggested the intemperate use of Mr. Freddy Alexander's pocket-handkerchief, but that were, in effect, produced by his struggle with a brand new hunting-horn. To this demonstration about as much attention was paid by the nine couple of buccaneers whom he was now exercising for the first time as might have been expected, and it was brought to abrupt conclusion by the sudden charge of two of them from the rear. Being coupled, they mowed his legs from under him as irresistibly as chain shot and being puppies, and of an imbecile friendliness they remained to lick his face and generally make merry over him as he struggled to his feet.

By this time the leaders of the pack were well away up a ploughed field, over a fence and into a furze brake, from which their rejoicing yelps streamed back on the damp breeze. The Master of the Craffroe Hounds picked himself up, and sprinted up the hill after the Whip and Kennel Huntsman--a composite official recently promoted from the stable yard--in a way that showed that his failure in horn-blowing was not the fault of his lungs. His feet were held by the heavy soil, he tripped in the muddy ridges; none the less he and Patsey plunged together over the stony rampart of the field in time to see Negress and Lily springing through the furze in kangaroo leaps, while they uttered long squeals of ecstasy. The rest of the pack, with a confidence gained in many a successful riot, got to them as promptly as if six Whips were behind them, and the whole faction plunged into a little wood on the top of what was evidently a burning scent.

"Was it a fox, Patsey?" said the Master excitedly.

"I dunno, Master Freddy: it might be 'twas a hare," returned Patsey, taking in a hurried reef in the strap that was responsible for the support of his trousers.

Freddy was small and light, and four short years before had been a renowned hare in his school paper-chases: he went through the wood at a pace that gave Patsey and the puppies all they could do to keep with him, and dropped into a road just in time to see the pack streaming up a narrow lane near the end of the wood. At this point they were reinforced by a yellow dachshund who, with wildly flapping ears, and at that caricature of a gallop peculiar to his kind, joined himself to the hunters.

"Glory be to Mercy!" exclaimed Patsey, "the misthress's dog!"

Almost simultaneously the pack precipitated themselves into a ruined cabin at the end of the lane; instantly from within arose an uproar of sounds--crashes of an ironmongery sort, yells of dogs, raucous human curses; then the ruin exuded hounds, hens and turkeys at every one of the gaps in its walls, and there issued from what had been the doorway a tall man with a red beard, armed with a large frying-pan, with which he rained blows on the fleeing Craffroe Pack. It must be admitted that the speed with which these abandoned their prey, whatever it was, suggested a very intimate acquaintance with the wrath of cooks and the perils of resistance.

Before their lawful custodians had recovered from this spectacle, a tall lady in black was suddenly merged in the *melee*, alternately calling loudly and incongruously for "Bismarck," and blowing shrill blasts on a whistle.

"If the tinker laves a sthroke of the pan on the misthress's dog, the Lord help him!" said Patsey, starting in pursuit of Lily, who, with tail tucked in and a wounded hind leg buckled up, was removing herself swiftly from the scene of action.

Mrs. Alexander shoved her way into the cabin, through a filthy group of gabbling male and female tinkers, and found herself involved in a wreck of branches and ragged tarpaulin that had once formed a kind of tent, but was now strewn on the floor by the incursion and excursion of the chase. Earthquake throes were convulsing the tarpaulin; a tinker woman, full of zeal, dashed at it and flung it back, revealing, amongst other *debris*, an old wooden bedstead heaped with rags. On either side of one of its legs protruded the passion-fraught faces of the coupled hound-puppies, who, still linked together, had passed through the period of unavailing struggle into a state of paralysed insanity of terror. Muffled squeals and tinny crashes told that conflict was still raging beneath the bed; the tinker women screamed abuse and complaint; and suddenly the dachshund's long yellow nose, streaming with blood, worked its way out of the folds. His mistress snatched at his collar and dragged him forth, and at his heels followed an infuriated tom cat, which, with its tail as thick as a muff, went like a streak through the confusion, and was lost in the dark ruin of the chimney.

Mrs. Alexander stayed for no explanations: she extricated herself from the tinker party, and, filled with a righteous wrath, went forth to look for her son. From a plantation three fields away came the asphyxiated bleats of the horn and the desolate bawls of Patsey Crimmeen. Mrs. Alexander decided that it was better for the present to leave the *personnel* of the Craffroe Hunt to their own devices.

It was but three days before these occurrences that Mr. Freddy Alexander had stood on the platform of the Craffroe Station, with a throbbing heart, and a very dirty paper in his hand containing a list of eighteen names, that ranged alphabetically from "Batchellor" to "Warior." At his elbow stood a small man with a large moustache, and the thinnest legs that were ever buttoned into gaiters, who was assuring him that to no other man in Ireland would he have sold those hounds at such a price; a statement that was probably unimpeachable.

"The only reason I'm parting them is I'm giving up me drag, and selling me stock, and going into partnership with a veterinary surgeon in Rugby. You've some of the best blood in Ireland in those hounds."

"Is it blood?" chimed in an old man who was standing, slightly drunk, at Mr. Alexander's other elbow. "The most of them hounds is by the Kerry Rapparee, and he was the last of the old Moynalty Baygles. Black dogs they were, with red eyes! Every one o' them as big as a yearling calf, and they'd hunt anything that'd roar before them!" He steadied himself on the new Master's arm. "I have them gethered in the ladies' waiting-room, sir, the way ye'll have no throuble. 'Twould be as good for ye to lave the muzzles on them till ye'll be through the town."

Freddy Alexander cannot to this hour decide what was the worst incident of that homeward journey; on the whole, perhaps, the most serious was the escape of Governess, who subsequently ravaged the country for two days, and was at length captured in the act of killing Mrs. Alexander's white Leghorn cock. For a young gentleman whose experience of hounds consisted in having learned at Cambridge to some slight and painful extent that if he rode too near them he got sworn at, the purchaser of the Kerry Rapparee's descendants had undertaken no mean task.

On the morning following on the first run of the Craffroe Hounds, Mrs. Alexander was sitting at her escritoire, making up her weekly accounts and entering in her poultry-book the untimely demise of the Leghorn cock. She was a lady of secret enthusiasms which sheltered themselves behind habits of the most business-like severity. Her books were models of order, and as she neatly inscribed the Leghorn cock's epitaph, "Killed by hounds," she could not repress the compensating thought that she had never seen Freddy's dark eyes and olive complexion look so well as when he had tried on his new pink coat.

At this point she heard a step on the gravel outside; Bismarck uttered a bloodhound bay and got under the sofa. It was a sunny morning in late October, and the French window was open; outside it, ragged as a Russian poodle and nearly as black, stood the tinker who had the day before wielded the frying-pan with such effect.

"Me lady," began the tinker, "I ax yer ladyship's pardon, but me little dog is dead."

"Well?" said Mrs. Alexander, fixing a gaze of clear grey rectitude upon him.

"Me lady," continued the tinker, reverentially but firmly, "'twas afther he was run by thim dogs yestherday, and 'twas your ladyship's dog that finished him. He tore the throat out of him under the bed!" He pointed an accusing forefinger at Bismarck, whose lambent eyes of terror glowed from beneath the valance of the sofa.

"Nonsense! I saw your dog; he was twice my dog's size," said Bismarck's mistress decidedly, not, however, without a remembrance of the blood on Bismarck's nose. She adored courage, and had always cherished a belief that Bismarck's shark-like jaws implied the possession of latent ferocity.

"Ah, but he was very wake, ma'am, afther he bein' hunted," urged the tinker. "I never slep' a wink the whole night, but keepin' sups o' milk to him and all sorts. Ah, ma'am, ye wouldn't like to be lookin' at him!"

The tinker was a very good-looking young man, almost apostolic in type, with a golden red aureole of hair and beard and candid blue eyes. These latter filled with tears as their owner continued:--

"He was like a brother for me; sure he follied me from home. 'Twas he was dam wise! Sure at home all me mother'd say to him was, "Where's the ducks, Captain?" an' he wouldn't lave wather nor bog-hole round the counthry but he'd have them walked and the ducks gethered. The pigs could be in their choice place, wherever they'd be he'd go around them. If ye'd tell him to put back the childhren from the fire, he'd ketch them by the sleeve and dhrag them."

The requiem ceased, and the tinker looked grievingly into his hat.

"What is your name?" asked Mrs. Alexander sternly. "How long is it since you left home?"

Had the tinker been as well acquainted with her as he was afterwards destined to become, he would have been aware that when she was most judicial she was frequently least certain of what her verdict was going to be.

"Me name's Willy Fennessy, me lady," replied the tinker, "an' I'm goin' the roads no more than three months. Indeed, me lady, I think the time too long that I'm with these blagyard thravellers. All the friends I have was poor Captain, and he's gone from me."

"Go round to the kitchen," said Mrs. Alexander.

The results of Willy Fennessy's going round to the kitchen were far-reaching. Its most immediate consequences were that (1) he mended the ventilator of the kitchen range; (2) he skinned a brace of rabbits for Miss Barnet, the cook; (3) he arranged to come next day and repair the clandestine devastations of the maids among the china.

He was pronounced to be a very agreeable young man.

Before luncheon (of which meal he partook in the kitchen) he had been consulted by Patsey Crimmeen about the chimney of the kennel boiler, had single-handed reduced it to submission, and had, in addition, boiled the meal for the hounds with a knowledge of proportion and an untiring devotion to the use of the potstick which produced "stirabout" of a smoothness and excellence that Miss Barnet herself might have been proud of.

"You know, mother," said Freddy that evening, "you do want another chap in the garden badly."

"Well it's not so much the garden," said Mrs. Alexander with alacrity, "but I think he might be very useful to you, dear, and it's such a great matter his being a teetotaler, and he seems so fond of animals. I really feel we ought to try and make up to him somehow for the loss of his dog; though, indeed, a more deplorable object than that poor mangy dog I never saw!"

"All right: we'll put him in the back lodge, and we'll give him Bizzy as a watch dog. Won't we, Bizzy?" replied Freddy, dragging the somnolent Bismarck from out of the heart of the hearthrug, and accepting without repugnance the comprehensive lick that enveloped his chin.

From which it may be gathered that Mrs. Alexander and her son had fallen, like their household, under the fatal spell of the fascinating tinker.

At about the time that this conversation was taking place, Mr. Fennessy, having spent an evening of valedictory carouse with his tribe in the ruined cottage, was walking, somewhat unsteadily, towards the wood, dragging after him by a rope a large dog. He did not notice that he was being followed by a barefooted woman, but the dog did, and, being an intelligent dog, was in some degree reassured. In the wood the tinker spent some time in selecting a tree with a projecting branch suitable to his purpose, and having found one he proceeded to hang the dog. Even in his cups Mr. Fennessy made sentiment subservient to common sense.

It is hardly too much to say that in a week the tinker had taken up a position in the Craffroe household only comparable to that of Ygdrasil, who in Norse mythology forms the ultimate support of all things. Save for the incessant demands upon his skill in the matter of solder and stitches, his recent tinkerhood was politely ignored, or treated as an escapade excusable in a youth of spirit. Had not his father owned a farm and seven cows in the county Limerick, and had not he himself three times returned the price of his ticket to America to a circle of adoring and wealthy relatives in Boston? His position in the kitchen and yard became speedily assured. Under his *regime* the hounds were valeted as they had never been before. Lily herself (newly washed, with "blue" in the water) was scarcely more white than the concrete floor of the kennel yard, and the puppies, Ruby and Remus, who had unaccountably developed a virulent form of mange, were immediately taken in hand by the all-accomplished tinker, and anointed with a mixture whose very noisomeness was to Patsey Crimmeen a sufficient guarantee of its efficacy, and was impressive even to the Master, fresh from much anxious study of veterinary lore.

"He's the best man we've got!" said Freddy proudly to a dubious uncle, "there isn't a mortal thing he can't put his hand to."

"Or lay his hands on," suggested the dubious uncle. "May I ask if his colleagues are still within a mile of the place?"

"Oh, he hates the very sight of 'em!" said Freddy hastily, "cuts 'em dead whenever he sees 'em."

"It's no use your crabbing him, George," broke in Mrs. Alexander, "we won't give him up to you! Wait till you see how he has mended the lock of the hall door!"

"I should recommend you to buy a new one at once," said Sir George Ker, in a way that was singularly exasperating to the paragon's proprietors.

Mrs. Alexander was, or so her friends said, somewhat given to vaunting herself of her paragons, under which heading, it may be admitted, practically all her household were included. She was, indeed, one of those persons who may or may not be heroes to their valets, but whose valets are almost invariably heroes to them. It was, therefore, excessively discomposing to her that, during the following week, in the very height of apparently cloudless domestic tranquillity, the housemaid and the parlour-maid should in one black hour successively demand an audience, and successively, in the floods of tears proper to such occasions, give warning. Inquiry as to their reasons was fruitless. They were unhappy: one said she wouldn't get her appetite, and that her mother was sick; the other said she wouldn't get her sleep in it, and there was things--sob--going on--sob.

Mrs. Alexander concluded the interview abruptly, and descended to the kitchen to interview her queen paragon, Barnet, on the crisis.

Miss Barnet was a stout and comely English lady, of that liberal forty that frankly admits itself in advertisements to be twenty-eight. It was understood that she had only accepted office in Ireland because, in the first place, the butler to whom she had long been affianced had married another, and because, in the second place, she had a brother buried in Belfast. She was, perhaps, the one person in the world whose opinion about poultry Mrs. Alexander ranked higher than her own. She now allowed a restrained acidity to mingle with her dignity of manner, scarcely more than the calculated lemon essence in her faultless castle puddings, but enough to indicate that she, too, had grievances. *She* didn't know why they were leaving. She had heard some talk about a fairy or something, but she didn't hold with such nonsense.

"Gerrls is very frightful!" broke in an unexpected voice; "owld standards like meself maybe wouldn't feel it!"

A large basket of linen had suddenly blocked the scullery door, and from beneath it a little woman, like an Australian aborigine, delivered herself of this dark saying.

"What are you talking about, Mrs. Griffen?" demanded Mrs. Alexander, turning in vexed bewilderment to her laundress, "what does all this mean?"

"The Lord save us, ma'am, there's some says it means a death in the house!" replied Mrs. Griffen with unabated cheerfulness, "an' indeed 'twas no blame for the little gerrls to be frightened an' they meetin' it in the passages--"

"Meeting *what*?" interrupted her mistress. Mrs. Griffen was an old and privileged retainer, but there were limits even for Mrs. Griffen.

"Sure, ma'am, there's no one knows what was in it," returned Mrs. Griffen, "but whatever it was they heard it goin' on before them always in the panthry passage, an' it walkin' as sthrong as a man. It whipped away up the stairs, and they seen the big snout snorting out at them through the banisters, and a bare back on it the same as a pig; and the two cheeks on it as white as yer own, and away with it! And with that Mary Anne got a wakeness, and only for Willy Fennessy bein' in the kitchen an' ketching a hold of her, she'd have cracked her head on the range, the crayture!"

Here Barnet smiled with ineffable contempt.

"What I'm tellin' them is," continued Mrs. Griffen, warming with her subject, "maybe that thing was a pairson that's dead, an' might be owin' a pound to another one, or has something that way on his soul, an' it's in the want o' some one that'll ax it what's throublin' it. The like o' thim couldn't spake till ye'll spake to thim first. But, sure, gerrls has no courage--"

Barnet's smile was again one of wintry superiority.

"Willy Fennessy and Patsey Crimmeen was afther seein' it too last night," went on Mrs. Griffen, "an' poor Willy was as much frightened! He said surely 'twas a ghost. On the back avenue it was, an' one minute 'twas as big as an ass, an' another minute it'd be no bigger than a bonnive--"

"Oh, the Lord save us!" wailed the kitchen-maid irrepressibly from the scullery.

"I shall speak to Fennessy myself about this," said Mrs. Alexander, making for the door with concentrated purpose, "and in the meantime I wish to hear no more of this rubbish."

"I'm sure Fennessy wishes to hear no more of it," said Barnet acridly to Mrs. Griffen, when Mrs. Alexander had passed swiftly out of hearing, "after the way those girls have been worryin' on at him about it all the morning. Such a set out!"

Mrs. Griffen groaned in a polite and general way, and behind Barnet's back put her tongue out of the corner of her mouth and winked at the kitchen-maid.

Mrs. Alexander found her conversation with Willy Fennessy less satisfactory than usual. He could not give any definite account of what he and Patsey had seen: maybe they'd seen nothing at all; maybe--as an obvious impromptu--it was the calf of the Kerry cow; whatever was in it, it was little he'd mind it, and, in easy dismissal of the subject, would the misthress be against his building a bit of a coal-shed at the back of the lodge while she was away?

That evening a new terror was added to the situation. Jimmy the boot-boy, on his return from taking the letters to the evening post, fled in panic into the kitchen, and having complied with the etiquette invariable in such cases by having "a wake-ness," he described to a deeply sympathetic audience how he had seen something that was like a woman in the avenue, and he had called to it and it returned him no answer, and how he had then asked it three times in the name o' God what was it, and it soaked away into the trees from him, and then there came something rushing in on him and grunting at him to bite him, and he was full sure it was the Fairy Pig from Lough Clure.

Day by day the legend grew, thickened by tales of lights that had been seen moving mysteriously in the woods of Craffroe. Even the hounds were subpoenaed as witnesses; Patsey Crimmeen's mother stating that for three nights after Patsey had seen that Thing they were singing and screeching to each other all night.

Had Mrs. Crimmeen used the verb scratch instead of screech she would have been nearer the mark. The puppies, Ruby and Remus, had, after the manner of the young, human and canine, not failed to distribute their malady among their elders, and the pack, straitly coupled, went for dismal constitutionals, and the kennels reeked to heaven of remedies, and Freddy's new hunter, Mayboy, from shortness of work, smashed the partition of the loose box and kicked his neighbour, Mrs. Alexander's cob, in the knee.

"The worst of it is," said Freddy confidentially to his ally and adviser, the junior subaltern of the detachment at Enniscar, who had come over to see the hounds, "that I'm afraid Patsey Crimmeen--the boy whom I'm training to whip to me, you know"--(as a matter of fact, the Whip was a year older than the Master)--"is begin-ning to drink a bit. When I came down here before breakfast this mornin'"--when Freddy was feeling more acutely than usual his position as an M.F.H., he cut his g's and talked slightly through his nose, even, on occasion, going so far as to omit the aspirate in talking of his hounds--"there wasn't a sign of him--kennel door not open or anything. I let the poor brutes out into the run. I tell you, what with the paraffin and the carbolic and everything the kennel was pretty high--"

"It's pretty thick now," said his friend, lighting a cigarette.

"Well, I went into the boiler-house," continued Freddy impressively, "and there he was, asleep on the floor, with his beastly head on my kennel coat, and one leg in the feeding trough!"

Mr. Taylour made a suitable ejaculation.

"I jolly soon kicked him on to his legs," went on Freddy, "not that they were much use to him--he must have been on the booze all night. After that I went on to the stable yard, and if you'll believe me, the two chaps there had never turned up at all--at half-past eight, mind you!--and there was Fennessy doing up the horses. He said he believed that there'd been a wake down at Enniscar last night. I thought it was rather decent of him doing their work for them."

"You'll sack 'em, I suppose?" remarked Mr. Taylour, with martial severity.

"Oh well, I don't know," said Mr. Alexander evasively, "I'll see. Anyhow, don't say anything to my mother about it; a drunken man is like a red rag to a bull to her."

Taking this peculiarity of Mrs. Alexander into consideration, it was perhaps as well that she left Craffroe a few days afterwards to stay with her brother. The eve-ning before she left both the Fairy Pig and the Ghost Woman were seen again on the avenue, this time by the coachman, who came into the kitchen considerably the worse for liquor and announced the fact, and that night the household duties were performed by the maids in pairs, and even, when possible, in trios.

As Mrs. Alexander said at dinner to Sir George, on the evening of her arrival, she was thankful to have abandoned the office of Ghostly Comforter to her domes-tics. Only for Barnet she couldn't have left poor Freddy to the mercy of that pack of fools; in fact, even with Barnet to look after them, it was impossible to tell what imbecility they were not capable of.

"Well, if you like," said Sir George, "I might run you over there on the motor car some day to see how they're all getting on. If Freddy is going to hunt on Friday, we might go on to Craffroe after seeing the fun."

The topic of Barnet was here shelved in favour of automobiles. Mrs. Alexander's brother was also a person of enthusiasms.

But what were these enthusiasms compared to the deep-seated ecstasy of Freddy Alexander as in his new pink coat he rode down the main street of Enniscar, Patsey in equal splendour bringing up the rear, unspeakably conscious of the jibes of his relatives and friends. There was a select field, consisting of Mr. Taylour, four farmers, some young ladies on bicycles, and about two dozen young men and boys on foot, who, in order to be prepared for all contingencies, had provided themselves with five dogs, two horns, and a ferret. It is, after all, impossible to please everybody, and from the cyclists' and foot people's point of view the weather left nothing to be desired. The sun shone like a glistering shield in the light blue November sky, the roads were like iron, the wind, what there was of it, like steel. There was a line of white on the northerly side of the fences, that yielded grudgingly and inch by inch before the march of the pale sunshine: the new pack could hardly have had a more unfavourable day for their *debut*.

The new Master was, however, wholly undaunted by such crumples in the rose-leaf. He was riding Mayboy, a big trustworthy horse, whose love of jumping had survived a month of incessant and arbitrary schooling, and he left the road as soon as was decently possible, and made a line across country for the covert that involved as much jumping as could reasonably be hoped for in half a mile. At the second fence Patsey Crimmeen's black mare put her nose in the air and swung round; Patsey's hands seemed to be at their worst this morning, and what their worst felt like the black mare alone knew. Mr. Taylour, as Deputy Whip, waltzed erratically round the nine couple on a very flippant polo pony; and the four farmers, who had wisely adhered to the road, reached the covert sufficiently in advance of the hunt to frustrate Lily's project of running sheep in a neighbouring field.

The covert was a large, circular enclosure, crammed to the very top of its girdling bank with furze-bushes, bracken, low hazel, and stunted Scotch firs. Its primary idea was woodcock, its second rabbits; beaters were in the habit of getting through it somehow, but a ride feasible for fox hunters had never so much as occurred to it. Into this, with practical assistance from the country boys, the deeply reluctant hounds were pitched and flogged; Freddy very nervously uplifted his voice in falsetto encouragement, feeling much as if he were starting the solo of an anthem; and Mr. Taylour and Patsey, the latter having made it up with the black mare, galloped away with professional ardour to watch different sides of the covert. This, during the next hour, they had ample opportunities for doing. After the first outburst of joy from the hounds on discovering that there were rabbits in the covert, and after the retirement of the rabbits to their burrows on the companion discovery that there were hounds in it, a silence, broken only by the far-away prattle of the lady bicyclists on the road, fell round Freddy Alexander. He bore it as long as he could, cheering with faltering whoops the invisible and unresponsive pack, and wondering what on earth huntsmen were expected to do on such occasions; then, filled with that horrid conviction which assails the lonely watcher, that the hounds have slipped away at the far side, he put spurs to Mayboy, and cantered down the long flank of the covert to find some one or something. Nothing had happened on the north side, at all events, for there was the faithful Taylour, pirouetting on his hill-top in the eye of the wind. Two fields more (in one of which he caught his first sight of any of the hounds, in the shape of Ruby, carefully rolling on a dead crow), and then, under the lee of a high bank, he came upon Patsey Crimmeen, the farmers, and the country boys, absorbed in the contemplation of a fight between Tiger, the butcher's brindled cur, and Watty, the kennel terrier.

The manner in which Mr. Alexander dispersed this entertainment showed that he was already equipped with one important qualification of a Master of Hounds--a temper laid on like gas, ready to blaze at a moment's notice. He pitched himself off his horse and scrambled over the bank into the covert in search of his hounds. He pushed his way through briars and furze-bushes, and suddenly, near the middle of the wood, he caught sight of them. They were in a small group, they were very quiet and very busy. As a matter of fact they were engaged in eating a dead sheep.

After this episode, there ensued a long and disconsolate period of wandering from one bleak hillside to another, at the bidding of various informants, in search of apocryphal foxes, slaughterers of flocks of equally apocryphal geese and turkeys--such a day as is discreetly ignored in all hunting annals, and, like the easterly wind that is its parent, is neither good for man nor beast.

By half-past three hope had died, even in the sanguine bosoms of the Master and Mr. Taylour. Two of the farmers had disappeared, and the lady bicyclists, with faces lavender blue from waiting at various windy cross roads, had long since fled away to lunch. Two of the hounds were limping; all, judging by their expressions, were on the verge of tears. Patsey's black mare had lost two shoes; Mr. Taylour's pony had ceased to pull, and was too dispirited even to try to kick the hounds, and the country boys had dwindled to four. There had come a time when Mr. Taylour had sunk so low as to suggest that a drag should be run with the assistance of the ferret's bag, a scheme only frustrated by the regrettable fact that the ferret and its owner had gone home.

"Well we had a nice bit of schooling, anyhow, and, it's been a real educational day for the hounds," said Freddy, turning in his saddle to look at the fires of the frosty sunset. "I'm glad they had it. I think we're in for a go of hard weather. I don't know what I should have done only for you, old chap. Patsey's gone all to pieces: it's my belief he's been on the drink this whole week, and where he gets it--"

"Hullo! Hold hard!" interrupted Mr. Taylour. "What's Governor after?"

They were riding along a grass-grown farm road outside the Craffroe demesne; the grey wall made a sharp bend to the right, and just at the corner Governor had begun to gallop, with his nose to the ground and his stern up. The rest of the pack joined him in an instant, and all swung round the corner and were lost to sight.

"It's a fox!" exclaimed Freddy, snatching up his reins; "they always cross into the demesne just here!"

By the time he and Mr. Taylour were round the corner the hounds had checked fifty yards ahead, and were eagerly hunting to and fro for the lost scent, and a little further down the old road they saw a woman running away from them.

"Hi, ma'am!" bellowed Freddy, "did you see the fox?"

The woman made no answer.

"Did you see the fox?" reiterated Freddy in still more stentorian tones. "Can't you answer me?"

The woman continued to run without even looking behind her.

The laughter of Mr. Taylour added fuel to the fire of Freddy's wrath: he put the spurs into Mayboy, dashed after the woman, pulled his horse across the road in front of her, and shouted his question point-blank at her, coupled with a warm inquiry as to whether she had a tongue in her head.

The woman jumped backwards as if she were shot, staring in horror at Freddy's furious little face, then touched her mouth and ears and began to jabber inarticulately and talk on her fingers.

The laughter of Mr. Taylour was again plainly audible.

"Sure that's a dummy woman, sir," explained the butcher's nephew, hurrying up. "I think she's one of them tinkers that's outside the town." Then with a long screech, "Look! Look over! Tiger, have it! Hulla, hulla, hulla!"

Tiger was already over the wall and into the demesne, neck and neck with Fly, the smith's half-bred greyhound; and in the wake of these champions clambered the Craffroe Pack, with strangled yelps of ardour, striving and squealing and fighting horribly in the endeavour to scramble up the tall smooth face of the wall.

"The gate! The gate further on!" yelled Freddy, thundering down the turfy road, with the earth flying up in lumps from his horse's hoofs.

Mr. Taylour's pony gave two most uncomfortable bucks and ran away; even Patsey Crimmeen and the black mare shared an unequal thrill of enthusiasm, as the latter, wholly out of hand, bucketed after the pony.

*   *   *   *   *

The afternoon was very cold, a fact thoroughly realised by Mrs. Alexander, on the front seat of Sir George's motor-car, in spite of enveloping furs, and of Bismarck, curled like a fried whiting, in her lap. The grey road rushed smoothly backwards under the broad tyres; golden and green plover whistled in the quiet fields, starlings and huge missel thrushes burst from the wayside trees as the "Bollee," uttering that hungry whine that indicates the desire of such creatures to devour space, tore past. Mrs. Alexander wondered if birds' beaks felt as cold as her nose after they had been cleaving the air for an afternoon; at all events, she reflected, they had not the consolation of tea to look forward to. Barnet was sure to have some of her best hot cakes ready for Freddy when he came home from hunting. Mrs. Alexander and Sir George had been scouring the roads since a very early lunch in search of the hounds, and her mind reposed on the thought of the hot cakes.

The front lodge gates stood wide open, the motor-car curved its flight and skimmed through. Half-way up the avenue they whizzed past three policemen, one of whom was carrying on his back a strange and wormlike thing.

"Janet," called out Sir George, "you've been caught making potheen! They've got the worm of a still there."

"They're only making a short cut through the place from the bog; I'm delighted they've found it!" screamed back Mrs. Alexander.

The "Bollee" was at the hall door in another minute, and the mistress of the house pulled the bell with numbed fingers. There was no response.

"Better go round to the kitchen," suggested her brother. "You'll find they're talking too hard to hear the bell."

His sister took the advice, and a few minutes afterwards she opened the hall door with an extremely perturbed countenance.

"I can't find a creature anywhere," she said, "either upstairs or down--I can't understand Barnet leaving the house empty--"

"Listen!" interrupted Sir George, "isn't that the hounds?"

They listened.

"They're hunting down by the back avenue! come on, Janet!"

The motor-car took to flight again; it sped, soft-footed, through the twilight gloom of the back avenue, while a disjointed, travelling clamour of hounds came nearer and nearer through the woods. The motor-car was within a hundred yards of the back lodge, when out of the rhododendron-bush burst a spectral black-and-white dog, with floating fringes of ragged wool and hideous bald patches on its back.

"Fennessy's dog!" ejaculated Mrs. Alexander, falling back in her seat.

Probably Bismarck never enjoyed anything in his life as much as the all too brief moment in which, leaning from his mistress's lap in the prow of the flying "Bollee," he barked hysterically in the wake of the piebald dog, who, in all its dolorous career had never before had the awful experience of being chased by a motor-car. It darted in at the open door of the lodge; the pursuers pulled up outside. There were paraffin lamps in the windows, the open door was garlanded with evergreens; from it proceeded loud and hilarious voices and the jerky strains of a concertina.

Mrs. Alexander, with all, her most cherished convictions toppling on their pedestals, stood in the open doorway and stared, unable to believe the testimony of her own eyes. Was that the immaculate Barnet seated at the head of a crowded table, in her--Mrs. Alexander's--very best bonnet and velvet cape, with a glass of steaming potheen punch in her hand, and Willy Fennessy's arm round her waist?

The glass sank from the paragon's lips, the arm of Mr. Fennessy fell from her waist; the circle of servants, tinkers, and country people vainly tried to efface themselves behind each other.

"Barnet!" said Mrs. Alexander in an awful voice, and even in that moment she appreciated with an added pang the feathery beauty of a slice of Barnet's sponge-cake in the grimy fist of a tinker.

"Mrs. Fennessy, m'm, if you please," replied Barnet, with a dignity that, considering the bonnet and cape, was highly creditable to her strength of character.

At this point a hand dragged Mrs. Alexander backwards from the doorway, a barefooted woman hustled past her into the house, slammed the door in her face, and Mrs. Alexander found herself in the middle of the hounds.

"We'd give you the brush, Mrs. Alexander," said Mr. Taylour, as he flogged solidly all round him in the dusk, "but as the other lady seems to have gone to ground with the fox I suppose she'll take it!"

*   *   *   *   *

Mrs. Fennessy paid out of her own ample savings the fines inflicted upon her husband for potheen-making and selling drink in the Craffroe gate lodge without a licence, and she shortly afterwards took him to America.

Mrs. Alexander's friends professed themselves as being not in the least surprised to hear that she had installed the afflicted Miss Fennessy (sister to the late occupant) and her scarcely less afflicted companion, the Fairy Pig, in her back lodge. Miss Fennessy, being deaf and dumb, is not perhaps a paragon lodge-keeper, but having, like her brother, been brought up in a work-house kitchen, she has taught Patsey Crimmeen how to boil stirabout *a merveille*.

FANNY FITZ'S GAMBLE

Where's Fanny Fitz?" said Captain Spicer to his wife.

They were leaning over the sea-wall in front of a little fishing ho-tel in Connemara, idling away the interval usually vouchsafed by the Irish car-driver between the hour at which he is ordered to be ready and that at which he appears. It was a misty morning in early June, the time of all times for Connemara, did the tourist only know it. The mountains towered green and grey above the palely shining sea in which they stood; the air was full of the sound of streams and the scent of wild flowers; the thin mist had in it something of the dazzle of the sunlight that was close behind it. Little Mrs. Spicer pulled down her veil: even after a fortnight's fly-fishing she still retained some regard for her complexion.

"She says she can't come," she responded; "she has letters to write or some-thing--and this is our last day!"

Mrs. Spicer evidently found the fact provoking.

"On this information the favourite receded 33 to 1," remarked Captain Spicer. "I think you may as well chuck it, my dear."

"I should like to beat them both!" said his wife, flinging a pebble into the rising tide that was very softly mouthing the seaweedy rocks below them.

"Well, here's Rupert; you can begin on him."

"Nothing would give me greater pleasure!" said Rupert's sister vindictively. "A great teasing, squabbling baby! Oh, how I hate fools! and they are **both** fools!--Oh, there you are, Rupert," a well-simulated blandness invading her voice; "and what's Fanny Fitz doing?"

"She's trying to do a Mayo man over a horse-deal," replied Mr. Rupert Gun-ning.

"A horse-deal!" repeated Mrs. Spicer incredulously. "Fanny buying a horse! Oh, impossible!"

"Well, I don't know about that," said Mr. Gunning, "she's trying pretty hard. I gave her my opinion--"

"I'll take my oath you did," observed Captain Spicer.

"--And as she didn't seem to want it, I came away," continued Mr. Gunning imperturbably. "Be calm, Maudie; it takes two days and two nights to buy a horse in these parts; you'll be home in plenty of time to interfere, and here's the car. Don't waste the morning."

"I never know if you're speaking the truth or no," complained Mrs. Spicer; nevertheless, she scrambled on to the car without delay. She and her brother had at least one point in common--the fanatic enthusiasm of the angler.

In the meantime, Miss Fanny Fitzroy's negotiations were proceeding in the hotel yard. Fanny herself was standing in a stable doorway, with her hands in the pockets of her bicycle skirt. She had no hat on, and the mild breeze blew her hair about; it was light brown, with a brightness in it; her eyes also were light brown, with gleams in them like the shallow places in a Connemara trout stream. At this moment they were scanning with approval, tempered by anxiety, the muddy legs of a lean and lengthy grey filly, who was fearfully returning her gaze from between the strands of a touzled forelock. The owner of the filly, a small man, with a face like a serious elderly monkey, stood at her head in a silence that was the outcome partly of stupidity, partly of caution, and partly of lack of English speech. The conduct of the matter was in the hands of a friend, a tall young man with a black beard, nimble of tongue and gesture, profuse in courtesies.

"Well, indeed, yes, your ladyship," he was saying glibly, "the breed of horses is greatly improving in these parts, and them hackney horses--"

"Oh," interrupted Miss Fitzroy hastily, "I won't have her if she's a hackney."

The eyes of the owner sought those of the friend in a gaze that clearly indicated the question.

"What'll ye say to her now?"

The position of the vendors was becoming a little complicated. They had come over through the mountains, from the borders of Mayo, to sell the filly to the hotel-keeper for posting, and were primed to the lips with the tale of her hackney lineage.

The hotel-keeper had unconditionally refused to trade, and here, when a heaven-sent alternative was delivered into their hands, they found themselves hampered by the coils of a cast-off lie. No shade, however, of hesitancy appeared on the open countenance of the friend. He approached Miss Fitzroy with a mincing step, a deprecating wave of the hand, and a deeply respectful ogle. He was going to adopt the desperate resource of telling the truth, but to tell the truth profitably was a part that required rather more playing than any other.

"Well, your honour's ladyship," he began, with a glance at the hotel ostler, who was standing near cleaning a bit in industrious and sarcastic silence, "it is a fact, no doubt, that I mentioned here this morning that this young mare was of the Government hackney stock. But, according as I understand from this poor man that owns her, he bought her in a small fair over the Tuam side, and the man that sold her could take his oath she was by the Grey Dawn--sure you'd know it out of her colour."

"Why didn't you say so before?" asked Miss Fitzroy, bending her straight brows in righteous severity.

"Well, that's true indeed, your ladyship; but, after all--I declare a man couldn't hardly live without he'd tell a lie sometimes!"

Fanny Fitz stooped, rather hurriedly, and entered upon a renewed examination of the filly's legs. Even Rupert Gunning, after his brief and unsympathetic survey, had said she had good legs; in fact, he had only been able to crab her for the length of her back, and he, as Fanny Fitz reflected with a heat that took no heed of metaphor, was the greatest crabber that ever croaked.

"What are you asking for her?" she demanded with a sudden access of decision.

There was a pause. The owner of the filly and his friend withdrew a step or two and conferred together in Irish at lightning speed. The filly held up her head and regarded her surroundings with guileless wonderment. Fanny Fitz made a mental dive into her bankbook, and arrived at the varied conclusions that she was L30 to the good, that on that sum she had to weather out the summer and autumn, besides pacifying various cormorants (thus she designated her long-suffering tradespeople), and that every one had told her that if she only kept her eyes open in Connemara she might be able to buy something cheap and make a pot of money on it.

"This poor honest man," said the friend, returning to the charge, "says he couldn't part her without he'd get twenty-eight pounds for her; and, thank God, it's little your ladyship would think of giving that!"

Fanny Fitz's face fell.

"Twenty-eight pounds!" she echoed. "Oh, that's ridiculous!"

The friend turned to the owner, and, with a majestic wave of the hand, signalled to him to retire. The owner, without a change of expression, coiled up the rope halter and started slowly and implacably for the gate; the friend took off his hat with wounded dignity. Every gesture implied that the whole transaction was buried in an irrevocable past.

Fanny Fitz's eyes followed the party as they silently left the yard, the filly stalking dutifully with a long and springy step beside her master. It was a moment full of bitterness, and of a quite irrational indignation against Rupert Gunning.

"I beg your pardon, miss," said the ostler, at her elbow, "would ye be willing to give twenty pounds for the mare, and he to give back a pound luck-penny?"

"I would!" said the impulsive Fanny Fitz, after the manner of her nation.

When the fishing party returned that afternoon Miss Fitzroy met them at the hall door.

"Well, my dear," she said airily to Mrs. Spicer, "what sort of sport have you had? I've enjoyed myself immensely. I've bought a horse!"

Mrs. Spicer sat, paralysed, on the seat of the outside car, disregarding her brother's outstretched hands.

"Fanny!" she exclaimed, in tones fraught with knowledge of her friend's resources and liabilities.

"Yes, I have!" went on Fanny Fitz, undaunted. "Mr. Gunning saw her. He said she was a long-backed brute. Didn't you, Mr. Gunning?"

Rupert Gunning lifted his small sister bodily off the car. He was a tall sallow man, with a big nose and a small, much-bitten, fair moustache.

"Yes, I believe I did," he said shortly.

Mrs. Spicer's blue eyes grew round with consternation.

"Then you really have bought the thing!" she cried. "Oh, Fanny, you idiot! And what on earth are you going to do with it?"

"It can sleep on the foot of my bed to-night," returned Fanny Fitz, "and I'll ride it into Galway to-morrow! Mr. Gunning, you can ride half-way if you like!"

But Mr. Gunning had already gone into the hotel with his rod and fishing basket. He had a gift, that he rarely lost a chance of exercising, of provoking Fanny Fitz to wrath, and the fact that he now declined her challenge may or may not be accounted for by the gloom consequent upon an empty fishing basket.

Next morning the various hangers-on in the hotel yard were provided with occupation and entertainment of the most satiating description. Fanny Fitz's new purchase was being despatched to the nearest railway station, some fourteen miles off. It had been arranged that the ostler was to drive her there in one of the hotel cars, which should then return with a horse that was coming from Galway for the hotel owner; nothing could have fitted in better. Unfortunately the only part of the arrangement that refused to fit in was the filly. Even while Fanny Fitz was finishing her toilet, high-pitched howls of objurgation were rising, alarmingly, from the stable-yard, and on reaching the scene of action she was confronted by the spectacle of the ostler being hurtled across the yard by the filly, to whose head he was clinging, while two helpers upheld the shafts of the outside car from which she had fled. All were shouting directions and warnings at the tops of their voices, the hotel dog was barking, the filly alone was silent, but her opinions were unmistakable.

A waiter in shirt-sleeves was leaning comfortably out of a window, watching the fray and offering airy suggestion and comment.

"It's what I'm telling them, miss," he said easily, including Fanny Fitz in the conversation; "if they get that one into Recess to-night it'll not be under a side-car."

"But the man I bought her from," said Fanny Fitz, lamentably addressing the company, "told me that he drove his mother to chapel with her last Sunday."

"Musha then, may the divil sweep hell with him and burn the broom afther!" panted the ostler in bitter wrath, as he slewed the filly to a standstill. "I wish himself and his mother was behind her when I went putting the crupper on her! B'leeve me, they'd drop their chat!"

"Sure I knew that young Geogheghan back in Westport," remarked the waiter, "and all the good there is about him was a little handy talk. Take the harness off her, Mick, and throw a saddle on her. It's little I'd think meself of canthering her into Recess!"

"How handy ye are yerself with your talk!" retorted the ostler; "it's canthering round the table ye'll be doing, and it's what'll suit ye betther!"

Fanny Fitz began to laugh. "He might ride the saddle of mutton!" she said, with a levity that, under the circumstances, did her credit. "You'd better take the harness off, and you'll have to get her to Recess for me somehow."

The ostler took no notice of this suggestion; he was repeating to himself: "Ride the saddle o' mutton! By dam, I never heard the like o' that! Ride the saddle o' mutton--!" He suddenly gave a yell of laughing, and in the next moment the startled filly dragged the reins from his hand with a tremendous plunge, and in half a dozen bounds was out of the yard gate and clattering down the road.

There was an instant of petrifaction. "Diddlety--iddlety--idlety!" chanted the waiter with far-away sweetness.

Fanny Fitz and the ostler were outside the gate simultaneously: the filly was already rounding the first turn of the road; two strides more, and she was gone as though she had never been, and "Oh, my nineteen pounds!" thought poor Fanny Fitz.

As the ostler was wont to say in subsequent repetitions of the story: "Thanks be to God, the reins was rotten!" But for this it is highly probable that Miss Fitz-roy's speculation would have collapsed abruptly with broken knees, possibly with a broken neck. Having galloped into them in the course of the first hundred yards, they fell from her as the green withes fell from Samson, one long streamer alone remaining to lash her flanks as she fled. Some five miles from the hotel she met a wedding, and therewith leaped the bog-drain by the side of the road and "took to the mountains," as the bridegroom poetically described it to Fanny Fitz, who, with the ostler, was pursuing the fugitive on an outside car.

"If that's the way," said the ostler, "ye mightn't get her again before the win-ther."

Fanny Fitz left the matter, together with a further instalment of the thirty pounds, in the hands of the sergeant of police, and went home, and, improbable as it may appear, in the course of something less than ten days she received an invoice from the local railway station, Enniscar, briefly stating: "1 horse arrd. Please remove."

Many people, most of her friends indeed, were quite unaware that Fanny Fitz possessed a home. Beyond the fact that it supplied her with a permanent address, and a place at which she was able periodically to deposit consignments of half-worn-out clothes, Fanny herself was not prone to rate the privilege very highly. Possibly, two very elderly maiden step-aunts are discouraging to the homing instinct; the fact remained that as long as the youngest Miss Fitzroy possessed the where-withal to tip a housemaid she was but rarely seen within the decorous precincts of Craffroe Lodge.

Let it not for a moment be imagined that the Connemara filly was to become a member of this household. Even Fanny Fitz, with all her optimism, knew better than to expect that William O'Loughlin, who divided his attentions between the ancient cob and the garden, and ruled the elder Misses Fitzroy with a rod of iron, would undertake the education of anything more skittish than early potatoes. It was to the stable, or rather cow-house, of one Johnny Connolly, that the new purchase was ultimately conveyed, and it was thither that Fanny Fitz, with apples in one pocket and sugar in the other, conducted her ally, Mr. Freddy Alexander, the master of the Craffroe Hounds. Fanny Fitz's friendship with Freddy was one of long standing, and was soundly based on the fact that when she had been eighteen he had been fourteen; and though it may be admitted that this is a discrepancy that somewhat fades with time, even Freddy's mother acquitted Fanny Fitz of any ulterior motive; and Freddy was an only son.

"She was very rejected last night afther she coming in," said Johnny Connolly, manipulating as he spoke the length of rusty chain and bit of stick that fastened the door. "I think it was lonesome she was on the thrain."

Fanny Fitz and Mr. Alexander peered into the dark and vasty interior of the cow-house; from a remote corner they heard a heavy breath and the jingle of a training bit, but they saw nothing.

"I have the cavesson and all on her ready for ye, and I was thinking we'd take her south into Mr. Gunning's land. His finces is very good," continued Johnny, going cautiously in; "wait till I pull her out."

Johnny Connolly was a horse trainer who did a little farming, or a farmer who did a little horse training, and his management of young horses followed no known rules, and indeed knew none, but it was generally successful. He fed them by rule of thumb; he herded them in hustling, squabbling parties in pitch-dark sheds; he ploughed them at eighteen months; he beat them with a stick like dogs when they transgressed, and like dogs they loved him. He had what gardeners call "a lucky hand" with them, and they throve with him, and he had, moreover, that gift of winning their wayward hearts that comes neither by cultivation nor by knowledge, but is innate and unconscious. Already, after two days, he and the Connemara filly understood each other; she sniffed distantly and with profound suspicion at Fanny and her offerings, and entirely declined to permit Mr. Alexander to estimate her height on the questionable assumption that the point of his chin represented 15'2, but she allowed Johnny to tighten or slacken every buckle in her new and unfamiliar costume without protest.

"I think she'll make a ripping good mare," said the enthusiastic Freddy, as he and Fanny Fitz followed her out of the yard; "I don't care what Rupert Gunning says, she's any amount of quality, and I bet you'll do well over her."

"She'll make a real nice fashionable mare," remarked Johnny, opening the gate of a field and leading the filly in, "and she's a sweet galloper, but she's very frightful in herself. Faith, I thought she'd run up the wall from me the first time I went to feed her! Ah ha! none o' yer thricks!" as the filly, becoming enjoyably aware of the large space of grass round her, let fling a kick of malevolent exuberance at the two fox-terriers who were trotting decorously in her rear.

It was soon found that, in the matter of "stone gaps," the A B C of Irish jumping, Connemara had taught the grey filly all there was to learn.

"Begor, Miss Fanny, she's as crabbed as a mule!" said her teacher approvingly. "D'ye mind the way she soaks the hind legs up into her! We'll give her a bank now."

At the bank, however, the trouble began. Despite the ministrations of Mr. Alexander and a long whip, despite the precept and example of Mr. Connolly, who performed prodigies of activity in running his pupil in at the bank and leaping on to it himself the filly time after time either ran her chest against it or swerved from it at the last instant with a vigour that plucked her preceptor from off it and scattered Fanny Fitz and the fox-terriers like leaves before the wind. These latter were divided between sycophantic and shrieking indignation with the filly for declining to jump, and a most wary attention to the sphere of influence of the whip. They were a mother and daughter, as conceited, as craven, and as wholly attractive as only the judiciously spoiled ladies of their race can be. Their hearts were divided between Fanny Fitz and the cook, the rest of them appertained to the Misses Harriet and Rachael Fitzroy, whom they regarded with toleration tinged with boredom.

"I tell ye now, Masther Freddy, 'tis no good for us to be goin' on sourin' the mare this way. 'Tis what the fince is too steep for her. Maybe she never seen the like in that backwards counthry she came from. We'll give her the bank below with the ditch in front of it. 'Tisn't very big at all, and she'll be bound to lep with the sup of wather that's in it."

Thus Johnny Connolly, wiping a very heated brow.

The bank below was a broad and solid structure well padded with grass and bracken, and it had a sufficiently obvious ditch, of some three feet wide, on the nearer side. The grand effort was duly prepared for. The bank was solemnly exhibited to the filly; the dogs, who had with unerring instinct seated themselves on its most jumpable portion, were scattered with one threat of the whip to the horizon. Fanny tore away the last bit of bracken that might prove a discouragement, and Johnny issued his final order.

"Come inside me with the whip, sir, and give her one good belt at the last."

No one knows exactly how it happened. There was a rush, a scramble, a backward sliding, a great deal of shouting, and the Connemara filly was couched in the narrow ditch at right angles to the fence, with the water oozing up through the weeds round her, like a wild duck on its nest; and at this moment Mr. Rupert Gunning appeared suddenly on the top of the bank and inspected the scene with an amusement that he made little attempt to conceal.

It took half an hour, and ropes, and a number of Rupert Gunning's haymakers, to get Fanny Fitz's speculation on to its legs again, and Mr. Gunning's comments during the process successfully sapped Fanny Fitz's control of her usually equable temper, "He's a beast!" she said wrathfully to Freddy, as the party moved soberly homewards in the burning June afternoon, with the horseflies clustering round them, and the smell of new-mown grass wafting to them from where, a field or two away, came the rattle of Rupert Gunning's mowing-machine. "A crabbing beast! It was just like my luck that he should come up at that moment and have the supreme joy of seeing Gamble--" Gamble was the filly's rarely-used name--"wallowing in the ditch! That's the second time he's scored off me. I *pity* poor little Maudie Spicer for having such a brother!"

In spite of this discouraging *debut*, the filly's education went on and prospered. She marched discreetly along the roads in long reins; she champed detested mouthfuls of rusty mouthing bit in the process described by Johnny Connolly as "getting her neck broke"; she trotted for treadmill half-hours in the lunge; and during and in spite of all these penances, she fattened up and thickened out until that great authority, Mr. Alexander, pronounced it would be a sin not to send her up to the Dublin Horse Show, as she was just the mare to catch an English dealer's eye.

"But sure ye wouldn't sell her, miss?" said her faithful nurse, "and Masther Freddy afther starting the hounds and all!"

Fanny Fitz scratched the filly softly under the jawbone, and thought of the document in her pocket--long, and blue, and inscribed with the too familiar notice in red ink: "An early settlement will oblige".

"I must, Johnny," she said, "worse luck!"

"Well, indeed, that's too bad, miss," said Johnny comprehendingly. "There was a mare I had one time, and I sold her before I went to America. God knows, afther she went from me, whenever I'd look at her winkers hanging on the wall I'd have to cry. I never seen a sight of her till three years afther that, afther I coming home. I was coming out o' the fair at Enniscar, an' I was talking to a man an' we coming down Dangan Hill, and what was in it but herself coming up in a cart! "An' I didn't look at her, good nor bad, nor know her, but sorra bit but she knew me talking, an' she turned in to me with the cart! Ho, ho, ho!' says she, and she stuck her nose into me like she'd be kissing me. Be dam, but I had to cry. An' the world wouldn't stir her out o' that till I'd lead her on meself. As for cow nor dog nor any other thing, there's nothing would rise your heart like a horse!"

*   *   *   *   *

It was early in July, a hot and sunny morning, and Fanny Fitz, seated on the flawless grassplot in front of Craffroe Lodge hall-door, was engaged in washing the dogs. The mother, who had been the first victim, was morosely licking herself, shuddering effectively, and coldly ignoring her oppressor's apologies. The daughter, trembling in every limb, was standing knee-deep in the bath; one paw, placed on its rim, was ready for flight if flight became practicable; her tail, rigid with anguish would have hummed like a violin-string if it were touched. Fanny, with her shirt-sleeves rolled up to her elbows, scrubbed in the soap. A clipped fuchsia hedge, the pride of William O'Loughlin's heart, screened the little lawn and garden from the high road.

"Good morning, Miss Fanny," said a voice over the hedge.

Fanny Fitz raised a flushed face and wiped a fleck of Naldyre off her nose with her arm.

"I've just been looking at your mare," went on the voice.

"Well, I hope you liked her!" said Fanny Fitz defiantly, for the voice was the voice of Rupert Gunning, and there was that in it that in this connection acted on Miss Fitzroy as a slogan.

"Well, 'like' is a strong word, you know!" said Mr. Gunning, moving on and standing with his arms on the top of the white gate and meeting Fanny's glance with provoking eyes. Then, as an after-thought, "Do you think you give her enough to eat?"

"She gets a feed of oats every Sunday, and strong tea and thistles through the week," replied Fanny Fitz in furious sarcasm.

"Yes, that's what she looks like," said Rupert Gunning thoughtfully. "Connolly tells me you want to send her to the show--Barnum's, I suppose--as the skeleton dude?"

"I believe you want to buy her yourself," retorted Fanny, with a vicious dab of the soap in the daughter's eye.

"Yes, she's just about up to my weight, isn't she? By-the-bye, you haven't had her backed yet, I believe?"

"I'm going to try her to-day!" said Fanny with sudden resolve.

"Ride her yourself!" said Mr. Gunning, his eyebrows going up into the roots of his hair.

"Yes!" said Fanny, with calm as icy as a sudden burst of struggles on the part of the daughter would admit of.

Rupert Gunning hesitated; then he said, "Well, she ought to carry a side-saddle well. Decent shoulders, and a nice long--" Perhaps he caught Fanny Fitz's eye; at all events, he left the commendation unfinished, and went on, "I should like to look in and see the performance, if I may? I suppose you wouldn't let me try her first? No?"

He walked on.

"Puppy, **will** you stay quiet!" said Fanny Fitz very crossly. She even slapped the daughter's soap-sud muffled person, for no reason that the daughter could see.

"Begorra, miss, I dunno," said Johnny Connolly dubiously when the suggestion that the filly should be ridden there and then was made to him a few minutes later; "wouldn't ye wait till I put her a few turns under the cart, or maybe threw a sack o' oats on her back?"

But Fanny would brook no delay. Her saddle was in the harness-room: William O'Loughlin could help to put it on; she would try the filly at once.

Miss Fitzroy's riding was of the sort that makes up in pluck what it wants in knowledge. She stuck on by sheer force of character; that she sat fairly straight, and let a horse's head alone were gifts of Providence of which she was wholly unconscious. Riding, in her opinion, was just getting on to a saddle and staying there, and making the thing under it go as fast as possible. She had always ridden other people's horses, and had ridden them so straight, and looked so pretty, that--other people in this connection being usually men--such trifles as riding out a hard run minus both fore shoes, or watering her mount generously during a check, were endured with a forbearance not frequent in horse owners. Hunting people, however, do not generally mount their friends, no matter how attractive, on young and valuable horses. Fanny Fitz's riding had been matured on well-seasoned screws, and she sallied forth to the subjugation of the Connemara filly with a self-confidence formed on experience only of the old, and the kind, and the cunning.

The filly trembled and sidled away from the garden-seat up to which Johnny Connolly had manoeuvred her. Johnny's supreme familiarity with young horses had brought him to the same point of recklessness that Fanny had arrived at from the opposite extreme, but some lingering remnant of prudence had induced him to put on the cavesson headstall, with the long rope attached to it, over the filly's bridle. The latter bore with surprising nerve Fanny's depositing of herself in the saddle.

"I'll keep a holt o' the rope, Miss Fanny," said Johnny, assiduously fondling his pupil; "it might be she'd be strange in herself for the first offer. I'll lead her on a small piece. Come on, gerr'l! Come on now!"

The pupil, thus adjured, made a hesitating movement, and Fanny settled herself down into the saddle. It was the shifting of the weight that seemed to bring home to the grey filly the true facts of the case, and with the discovery she shot straight up into the air as if she had been fired from a mortar. The rope whistled through Johnny Connolly's fingers, and the point of the filly's shoulder laid him out on the ground with the precision of a prize-fighter.

"I felt, my dear," as Fanny Fitz remarked in a letter to a friend, "as if I were in something between an earthquake and a bad dream and a churn. I just ***clamped*** my legs round the crutches, and she whirled the rest of me round her like the lash of a whip. In one of her flights she nearly went in at the hall door, and I was aware of William O'Loughlin's snow-white face somewhere behind the geraniums in the porch. I think I was clean out of the saddle then. I remember looking up at my knees, and my left foot was nearly on the ground. Then she gave another flourish, and swung me up on top again. I was hanging on to the reins hard; in fact, I think they must have pulled me back on to the saddle, as I ***know*** at one time I was sitting in a bunch on the stirrup! Then I heard most heart-rending yells from the poor old Aunts: 'Oh, the begonias! O Fanny, get off the grass!' and then, suddenly, the filly and I were perfectly still, and the house and the trees were spinning round me, black, edged with green and yellow dazzles. Then I discovered that some one had got hold of the cavesson rope and had hauled us in, as if we were salmon; Johnny had grabbed me by the left leg, and was trying to drag me off the filly's back; William O'Loughlin had broken two pots of geraniums, and was praying loudly among the fragments; and Aunt Harriet and Aunt Rachel, who don't to this hour realise that anything unusual had happened, were reproachfully collecting the trampled remnants of the begonias."

It was, perhaps unworthy on Fanny Fitz's part to conceal the painful fact that it was that distinguished fisherman, Mr. Rupert Gunning, who had landed her and the Connemara filly. Freddy Alexander, however, heard the story in its integrity, and commented on it with his usual candour. "I don't know which was the bigger fool, you or Johnny," he said; "I think you ought to be jolly grateful to old Rupert!"

"Well, I'm not!" returned Fanny Fitz.

After this episode the training of the filly proceeded with more system and with entire success. Her nerves having been steadied by an hour in the lunge with a sack of oats strapped, Mazeppa-like, on to her back, she was mounted without difficulty, and was thereafter ridden daily. By the time Fanny's muscles and joints had recovered from their first attempt at rough-riding, the filly was taking her place as a reasonable member of society, and her nerves, which had been as much *en evidence* as her bones, were, like the latter, finding their proper level, and becoming clothed with tranquillity and fat. The Dublin Horse Show drew near, and, abetted by Mr. Alexander, Fanny Fitz filled the entry forms and drew the necessary cheque, and then fell back in her chair and gazed at the attentive dogs with fateful eyes.

"Dogs!" she said, "if I don't sell the filly I am done for!"

The mother scratched languidly behind her ear till she yawned musically, but said nothing. The daughter, who was an enthusiast, gave a sudden bound on to Miss Fitzroy's lap, and thus it was that the cheque was countersigned with two blots and a paw mark.

None the less, the bank honoured it, being a kind bank, and not desirous to emphasise too abruptly the fact that Fanny Fitz was overdrawn.

In spite of, or rather, perhaps, in consequence of this fact, it would have been hard to find a smarter and more prosperous-looking young woman than the owner of No. 548, as she signed her name at the season-ticket turnstile and entered the wide soft aisles of the cathedral of horses at Ballsbridge. It was the first day of the show, and in token of Fanny Fitz's enthusiasm be it recorded, it was little more than 9.30 A.M. Fanny knew the show well, but hitherto only in its more worldly and social aspects. Never before had she been of the elect who have a horse "up," and as she hurried along, attended by Captain Spicer, at whose house she was staying, and Mr. Alexander, she felt magnificently conscious of the importance of the position.

The filly had preceded her from Craffroe by a couple of days, under the charge of Patsey Crimmeen, lent by Freddy for the occasion.

"I don't expect a prize, you know," Fanny had said loftily to Mr. Gunning, "but she has improved so tremendously, every one says she ought to be an easy mare to sell."

The sun came filtering through the high roof down on to the long rows of stalls, striking electric sparks out of the stirrup-irons and bits, and adding a fresh gloss to the polish that the grooms were giving to their charges. The judging had begun in several of the rings, and every now and then a glittering exemplification of all that horse and groom could be would come with soft thunder up the tan behind Fanny and her squires.

"We've come up through the heavy weights," said Captain Spicer; "the twelve-stone horses will look like rats--" He stopped.

They had arrived at the section in which figured "No. 548. Miss F. Fitzroy's 'Gamble,' grey mare; 4 years, by Grey Dawn," and opposite them was stall No. 548. In it stood the Connemara filly, or rather something that might have been her astral body. A more spectral, deplorable object could hardly be imagined. Her hind quarters had fallen in, her hips were standing out; her ribs were like the bars of a grate; her head, hung low before her, was turned so that one frightened eye scanned the passers-by, and she propped her fragile form against the partition of her stall, as though she were too weak to stand up.

To say that Fanny Fitz's face fell is to put it mildly. As she described it to Mrs. Spicer, it fell till it was about an inch wide and five miles long. Captain Spicer was speechless. Freddy alone was equal to demanding of Patsey Crimmeen what had happened to the mare.

"Begor, Masther Freddy, it's a wonder she's alive at all!" replied Patsey, who was now perceived to be looking but little better than the filly. "She was middlin' quiet in the thrain, though she went to lep out o' the box with the first screech the engine give, but I quietened her some way, and it wasn't till we got into the sthreets here that she went mad altogether. Faith, I thought she was into the river with me three times! 'Twas hardly I got her down the quays; and the first o' thim alechtric thrams she seen! Look at me hands, sir! She had me swingin' on the rope the way ye'd swing a flail. I tell you, Masther Freddy, them was the ecstasies!"

Patsey paused and gazed with a gloomy pride into the stricken faces of his audience.

"An' as for her food," he resumed, "she didn't use a bit, hay, nor oats, nor bran, bad nor good, since she left Johnny Connolly's. No, nor drink. The divil dang the bit she put in her mouth for two days, first and last. Why wouldn't she eat is it, miss? From the fright sure! She'll do nothing, only standing that way, and bushtin' out sweatin', and watching out all the time the way I wouldn't lave her. I declare to God

I'm heart-scalded with her!"

At this harrowing juncture came the order to No. 548 to go forth to Ring 3 to be judged, and further details were reserved. But Fanny Fitz had heard enough.

"Captain Spicer," she said, as the party paced in deepest depression towards Ring 3, "if I hadn't on a new veil I should cry!"

"Well, I haven't," replied Captain Spicer; "shall I do it for you? Upon my soul, I think the occasion demands it!"

"I just want to know one thing," continued Miss Fitzroy. "When does your brother-in-law arrive?"

"Not till to-night."

"That's the only nice thing I've heard to-day," sighed Fanny Fitz.

The judging went no better for the grey filly than might have been expected, even though she cheered up a little in the ring, and found herself equal to an invalidish but well-aimed kick at a fellow-competitor. She was ushered forth with the second batch of the rejected, her spirits sank to their former level, and Fanny's accompanied them.

Perhaps the most trying feature of the affair was the reproving sympathy of her friends, a sympathy that was apt to break down into almost irrepressible laughter at the sight of the broken-down skeleton of whose prowess poor Fanny Fitz had so incautiously boasted.

"Y' know, my dear child," said one elderly M.F.H., "you had no business to send up an animal without the condition of a wire fence to the Dublin Show. Look at my horses! Fat as butter, every one of 'em!"

"So was mine, but it all melted away in the train," protested Fanny Fitz in vain. Those of her friends who had only seen the mare in the catalogue sent dealers to buy her, and those who had seen her in the flesh--or what was left of it--sent amateurs; but all, dealers and the greenest of amateurs alike, entirely declined to think of buying her.

The weather was perfect; every one declared there never was a better show, and Fanny Fitz, in her newest and least-paid-for clothes, looked brilliantly successful, and declared to Mr. Rupert Gunning that nothing made a show so interesting as having something up for it. She even encouraged him to his accustomed jibes at her Connemara speculation, and personally conducted him to stall No. 548, and made merry over its melancholy occupant in a way that scandalised Patsey, and convinced Mrs. Spicer that Fanny's pocket was even harder hit than she had feared.

On the second day, however, things looked a little more hopeful.

"She ate her grub last night and this morning middlin' well, miss," said Patsey, "and"--here he looked round stealthily and began to whisper--"when I had her in the ring, exercisin', this morning, there was one that called me in to the rails; like a dealer he was. 'Hi! grey mare!' says he. I went in. 'What's your price?' says he. 'Sixty guineas, sir,' says I. 'Begin at the shillings and leave out the pounds!' says he. He went away then, but I think he's not done with me."

"I'm sure the ring is our best chance, Patsey," said Fanny, her voice thrilling with the ardour of conspiracy and of reawakened hope. "She doesn't look so thin when she's moving. I'll go and stand by the rails, and I'll call you in now and then just to make people look at her!"

"Sure I had Masther Freddy doing that to me yestherday," said Patsey; but hope dies hard in an Irishman, and he saddled up with all speed.

For two long burning hours did the Connemara filly circle in Ring 3, and during all that time not once did her owner's ears hear the longed-for summons, "Hi! grey mare!" It seemed to her that every other horse in the ring was called in to the rails, "and she doesn't look so very thin to-day!" said Fanny indignantly to Captain Spicer, who, with Mr. Gunning, had come to take her away for lunch.

"Oh, you'll see, you'll sell her on the last day; she's getting fitter every minute," responded Captain Spicer. "What would you take for her?"

"I'm asking sixty," said Fanny dubiously. "What would *you* take for her, Mr. Gunning--on the last day, you know?"

"I'd take a ticket for her," said Rupert Gunning, "back to Craffroe--if you haven't a return."

The second and third days crawled by unmarked by any incident of cheer, but on the morning of the fourth, when Fanny arrived at the stall, she found that Patsey had already gone out to exercise. She hurried to the ring and signalled to him to come to her.

"There's a fella' afther her, miss!" said Patsey, bending very low and whispering at close and tobacco-scented range. "He came last night to buy her; a jock he was, from the Curragh, and he said for me to be in the ring this morning. He's not come yet. He had a straw hat on him."

Fanny sat down under the trees and waited for the jockey in the straw hat. All around were preoccupied knots of bargainers, of owners making their final arrangements, of would-be-buyers hurrying from ring to ring in search of the paragon that they had now so little time to find. But the man from the Curragh came not. Fanny sent the mare in, and sat on under the trees, sunk in depression. It seemed to her she was the only person in the show who had nothing to do, who was not clinking handfuls of money, or smoothing out banknotes, or folding up cheques and interring them in fat and greasy pocket-books. She had never known this aspect of the Horse Show before, and--so much is in the point of view--it seemed to her sordid and detestable. Prize-winners with their coloured rosettes were swaggering about everywhere. Every horse in the show seemed to have got a prize except hers, thought Fanny. And not a man in a straw hat came near Ring 3.

She went home to lunch, dead tired. The others were going to see the polo in the park.

"I must go back and sell the mare," said Fanny valiantly, "or else take that ticket to Craffroe, Mr. Gunning!"

"Well, we'll come down and pick you up there after the first match, you poor, miserable thing," said Mrs. Spicer, "and I hope you'll find that beast of a horse dead when you get there! You look half dead yourself!"

How sick Fanny was of signing her name at that turnstile! The pen was more atrocious every time. How tired her feet were! How sick she was of the whole thing, and how incredibly big a fool she had been! She was almost too tired to know what she was doing, and she had actually walked past stall No. 548 without noticing it, when she heard Patsey's voice calling her.

"Miss Fanny! Miss Fanny! I have her sold! The mare's sold, miss! See here! I have the money in me pocket!"

The colour flooded Fanny Fitz's face. She stared at Patsey with eyes that more than ever suggested the Connemara trout-stream with the sun playing in it; so bright were they, so changing, and so wet. So at least thought a man, much addicted to fishing, who was regarding the scene from a little way off.

"He was a dealer, miss," went on Patsey; "a Dublin fella'. Sixty-three sovereigns I asked him, and he offered me fifty-five, and a man that was there said we should shplit the differ, and in the latther end he gave me the sixty pounds. He wasn't very stiff at all. I'm thinking he wasn't buying for himself."

The man who had noticed Fanny Fitz's eyes moved away unostentatiously. He had seen in them as much as he wanted; for that time at least.

THE CONNEMARA MARE

PART I

The grey mare who had been one of the last, if not the very last, of the sales at the Dublin Horse Show, was not at all happy in her mind.

Still less so was the dealer's under-strapper, to whom fell the task of escorting her through the streets of Dublin. Her late owner's groom had assured him that she would "folly him out of his hand, and that whatever she'd see she wouldn't care for it nor ask to look at it!"

It cannot be denied, however, that when an electric tram swept past her like a terrace under weigh, closely followed by a cart laden with a clanking and horrific reaping-machine, she showed that she possessed powers of observation. The incident passed off with credit to the under-strapper, but when an animal has to be played like a salmon down the length of Lower Mount Street, and when it barn-dances obliquely along the north side of Merrion Square, the worst may be looked for in Nassau Street.

And it was indeed in Nassau Street, and, moreover, in full view of the bow window of Kildare Street Club, that the cup of the under-strapper's misfortunes brimmed over. To be sure he could not know that the new owner of the grey mare was in that window; it was enough for him that a quiescent and unsuspected piano-organ broke with three majestic chords into Mascagni's "Intermezzo" at his very ear, and that, without any apparent interval of time, he was surmounting a heap composed of a newspaper boy, a sandwich man, and a hospital nurse, while his hands held nothing save a red-hot memory of where the rope had been. The smashing of glass and the clatter of hoofs on the pavement filled in what space was left in his mind for other impressions.

"She's into the hat shop!" said Mr. Rupert Gunning to himself in the window of the club, recognising his recent purchase and the full measure of the calamity in one and the same moment.

He also recognised in its perfection the fact, already suspected by him, that he had been a fool.

Upheld by this soothing reflection he went out into the street, where awaited him the privileges of proprietorship. These began with the despatching of the mare, badly cut, and apparently lame on every leg, in charge of the remains of the understrapper, to her destination. They continued with the consolation of the hospital nurse, and embraced in varying pecuniary degrees the compensation of the sandwich man, the newspaper boy, and the proprietor of the hat shop. During all this time he enjoyed the unfaltering attention of a fair-sized crowd, liberal in comment, prolific of imbecile suggestion. And all these things were only the beginning of the trouble.

Mr. Gunning proceeded to his room and to the packing of his portmanteau for that evening's mail-boat to Holyhead in a mood of considerable sourness. It may be conceded to him that circumstances had been of a souring character. He had bought Miss Fanny Fitzroy's grey mare at the Horse Show for reasons of an undeniably sentimental sort. Therefore, having no good cause to show for the purchase, he had made it secretly, the sum of sixty pounds, for an animal that he had consistently crabbed, amounting in the eyes of the world in general to a rather advanced love-token, if not a formal declaration. He had planned no future for the grey mare, but he had cherished a trembling hope that some day he might be in a position to restore her to her late owner without considering the expression in any eyes save those which, a couple of hours ago, had recalled to him the play of lights in a Connemara trout stream.

Now, it appeared, this pleasing vision must go the way of many others.

The August sunlight illumined Mr. Gunning's folly, and his bulging portmanteau, packed as brutally as only a man in a passion can pack; when he reached the hall, it also with equal inappropriateness irradiated the short figure and seedy tidiness of the dealer who had been his confederate in the purchase of the mare.

"What did the vet say, Brennan?" said Mr. Gunning, with the brevity of ill humour.

Mr. Brennan paused before replying, a pause laden with the promise of evil tidings. His short silvery hair glistened respectably in the sunshine: he had preserved unblemished from some earlier phase of his career the air of a family coachman out of place. It veiled, though it could not conceal, the dissolute twinkle in his eye as he replied:--

"He said sir, if it wasn't that she was something out of condition, he'd recommend you to send her out to the lions at the Zoo!"

The specimen of veterinary humour had hardly the success that had been hoped for it. Rupert Gunning's face was so remarkably void of appreciation that Mr. Brennan abruptly relapsed into gloom.

"He said he'd only be wasting his time with her, sir; he might as well go stitch a bog-hole as them wounds the window gave her; the tendon of the near fore is the same as in two halves with it, let alone the shoulder, that's worse again with her pitching out on the point of it."

"Was that all he had to say?" demanded the mare's owner.

"Well, beyond those remarks he passed about the Zoo, I should say it was, sir," admitted Mr. Brennan.

There was another pause, during which Rupert asked himself what the devil he was to do with the mare, and Mr. Brennan, thoroughly aware that he was doing so, decorously thumbed the brim of his hat.

"Maybe we might let her get the night, sir," he said, after a respectful interval, "and you might see her yourself in the morning--"

"I don't want to see her. I know well enough what she looks like," interrupted his client irritably. "Anyhow, I'm crossing to England to-night, and I don't choose to miss the boat for the fun of looking at an unfortunate brute that's cut half to pieces!"

Mr. Brennan cleared his throat. "If you were thinking to leave her in my stables, sir," he said firmly, "I'd sooner be quit of her. I've only a small place, and I'd lose too much time with her if I had to keep her the way she is. She might be on my hands three months and die at the end of it."

The clock here struck the quarter, at which Mr. Gunning ought to start for his train at Westland Row.

"You see, sir--" recommenced Brennan. It was precisely at this point that Mr. Gunning lost his temper.

"I suppose you can find time to shoot her," he said, with a very red face. "Kindly do so to-night!"

Mr. Brennan's arid countenance revealed no emotion. He was accustomed to understanding his clients a trifle better than they understood themselves, and inscrutable though Mr. Gunning's original motive in buying the mare had been, he had during this interview yielded to treatment and followed a prepared path.

That night, in the domestic circle, he went so far as to lay the matter before Mrs. Brennan.

"He picked out a mare that was as poor as a raven--though she's a good enough stamp if she was in condition--and tells me to buy her. 'What price will I give, sir?' says I. 'Ye'll give what they're askin',' says he, 'and that's sixty sovereigns!' I'm thirty years buying horses, and such a disgrace was never put on me, to be made a fool of before all Dublin! Going giving the first price for a mare that wasn't value for the half of it! Well; he sees the mare then, cut into garters below in Nassau Street. Devil a hair he cares! Nor never came down to the stable to put an eye on her! 'Shoot her!' says he, leppin' up on a car. 'Westland Row!' says he to the fella'. 'Drive like blazes!' and away with him! Well, no matter; I earned my money easy, an' I got the mare cheap!"

Mrs. Brennan added another spoonful of brown sugar to the porter that she was mulling in a sauce-pan on the range.

"Didn't ye say it was a young lady that owned the mare, James?" she asked in a colourless voice.

"Well, you're the devil, Mary!" replied Mr. Brennan in sincere admiration.

The mail-boat was as crowded as is usual on the last night of the Horse Show week. Overhead flowed the smoke river from the funnels, behind flowed the foam river of wake; the Hill of Howth receded apace into the west, and its lighthouse glowed like a planet in the twilight. Men with cigars, aggressively fit and dinner-full, strode the deck in couples, and thrashed out the Horse Show and Leopardstown to their uttermost husks.

Rupert Gunning was also, but with excessive reluctance, discussing the Horse Show. As he had given himself a good deal of trouble in order to cross on this particular evening, and as any one who was even slightly acquainted with Miss Fitzroy must have been aware that she would decline to talk of anything else, sympathy for him is not altogether deserved. The boat swung softly in a trance of speed, and Miss Fitzroy, better known to a large circle of intimates as Fanny Fitz, tried to think the motion was pleasant. She had made a good many migrations to England, by various routes and classes. There had indeed been times of stress when she had crossed unostentatiously, third class, trusting that luck and a thick veil might save her from her friends, but the day after she had sold a horse for sixty pounds was not the day for a daughter of Ireland to study economics. The breeze brought warm and subtle wafts from the machinery; it also blew wisps of hair into Fanny Fitz's eyes and over her nose, in a manner much revered in fiction, but in real life usually unbecoming and always exasperating. She leaned back on the bench and wondered whether the satisfaction of crowing over Mr. Gunning compensated her for abandoning the tranquil security of the ladies' cabin.

Mr. Gunning, though less contradictious than his wont, was certainly one of the most deliberately unsympathetic men she knew. None the less he was a man, and some one to talk to, both points in his favour, and she stayed on.

"I just missed meeting the man who bought my mare," she said, recurring to the subject for the fourth time; "apparently *he* didn't think her 'a leggy, long-backed brute,' as other people did, or said they did!"

"Did many people say it?" asked Mr. Gunning, beginning to make a cigarette.

"Oh, no one whose opinion signified!" retorted Fanny Fitz, with a glance from her charming, changeful eyes that suggested that she did not always mean quite what she said. "I believe the dealer bought her for a Leicestershire man. What she really wants is a big country where she can extend herself."

Mr. Gunning reflected that by this time the grey mare had extended herself once for all in Brennan's back-yard: he had done nothing to be ashamed of, but he felt abjectly guilty.

"If I go with Maudie to Connemara again next year," continued Fanny, "I must look out for another. You'll come too, I hope? A little opposition is such a help in making up one's mind! I don't know what I should have done without you at Leenane last June!"

Perhaps it was the vision of early summer that the words called up; perhaps it was the smile, half-seen in the semi-dark, that curved her provoking lips; perhaps it was compunction for his share in the tragedy of the Connemara mare; but possibly without any of these explanations Rupert would have done as he did, which was to place his hand on Fanny Fitz's as it lay on the bench beside him.

She was so amazed that for a moment she wildly thought he had mistaken it in the darkness for his tobacco pouch. Then, jumping with a shock to the conclusion that even the unsympathetic Mr. Gunning shared most men's views about not wasting an opportunity, she removed her hand with a jerk.

"Oh! I beg your pardon!" said Rupert pusillanimously. Miss Fitzroy fell back again on the tobacco pouch theory.

At this moment the glowing end of a cigar deviated from its orbit on the deck and approached them.

"Is that you, Gunning? I thought it was your voice," said the owner of the cigar.

"Yes, it is," said Mr. Gunning, in a tone singularly lacking in encouragement. "Thought I saw you at dinner, but couldn't be sure."

As a matter of fact, no one could have been more thoroughly aware than he of Captain Carteret's presence in the saloon.

"I thought so too!" said Fanny Fitz, from the darkness, "Captain Carteret wouldn't look my way!"

Captain Carteret gave a somewhat exaggerated start of discovery, and threw his cigar over the side. He had evidently come to stay.

"How was it I didn't see you at the Horse Show?" he said.

"The only people one ever sees there are the people one doesn't want to see," said Fanny, "I could meet no one except the auctioneer from Craffroe, and he always said the same thing. 'Fearful sultry, Miss Fitzroy! Have ye a purchaser yet for your animal, Miss Fitzroy? Ye have not! Oh, fie, fie!' It was rather funny at first, but it palled."

"I was only there one day," said Captain Carteret; "I wish I'd known you had a horse up, I might have helped you to sell."

"Thanks! I sold all right," said Fanny Fitz magnificently. "Did rather well too!"

"Capital!" said Captain Carteret vaguely. His acquaintance with Fanny extended over a three-day shooting party in Kildare, and a dance given by the detachment of his regiment at Enniscar, for which he had come down from the depot. It was not sufficient to enlighten him as to what it meant to her to own and sell a horse for the first time in her life.

"By-the-bye, Gunning," he went on, "you seemed to be having a lively time in Nassau Street yesterday! My wife and I were driving in from the polo, and we saw you in the thick of what looked like a street row. Some one in the club afterwards told me it was a horse you had only just bought at the Show that had come to grief. I hope it wasn't much hurt?"

There was a moment of silence--astonished, inquisitive silence on the part of Miss Fitzroy temporary cessation of the faculty of speech on that of Mr. Gunning. It was the moment, as he reflected afterwards, for a clean, decisive lie, a denial of all ownership; either that, or the instant flinging of Captain Carteret overboard.

Unfortunately for him, he did neither; he lied partially, timorously, and with that clinging to the skirts of the truth that marks the novice.

"Oh, she was all right," he said, his face purpling heavily in the kindly darkness. "What was the polo like, Carteret?"

"But I had no idea that you had bought a horse!" broke in Fanny Fitz, in high excitement. "Why didn't you tell Maudie and me? What is it like?"

"Oh, it's--she's just a cob--a grey cob--I just picked her up at the end of the show."

"What sort of a cob? Can she jump? Are you going to ride her with Freddy's hounds?" continued the implacably interested Fanny.

"I bought her as--as a trapper, and to do a bit of carting," replied Rupert, beginning suddenly to feel his powers of invention awakening; "she's quite a common brute. She doesn't jump."

"She seems to have jumped pretty well in Nassau Street," remarked Captain Carteret; "as well as I could see in the crowd, she didn't strike me as if she'd take kindly to carting."

"Well, I do think you might have told us about it!" reiterated Fanny Fitz. "Men are so ridiculously mysterious about buying or selling horses. I simply named my price and got it. *I* see nothing to make a mystery about in a deal; do you, Captain Carteret?"

"Well, that depends on whether you are buying or selling," replied Captain

Carteret.

But Fate, in the shape of a turning tide and a consequent roll, played for once into the hands of Rupert Gunning. The boat swayed slowly, but deeply, and a waft of steam blew across Miss Fitzroy's face. It was not mere steam; it had been among hot oily things, stealing and giving odour. Fanny Fitz was not ill, but she knew that she had her limits, and that conversation, save of the usual rudimentary kind with the stewardess, were best abandoned.

Miss Fitzroy's movements during the next two and a half months need not be particularly recorded. They included--

1. A week in London, during which the sixty pounds, or a great part of it, acquired by the sale of the Connemara mare, passed imperceptibly into items, none of which, on a strict survey of expenditure, appeared to exceed three shillings and nine pence.

2. A month at Southsea, with Rupert Gunning's sister, Maudie Spicer, where she again encountered Captain Carteret, and entered aimlessly upon a semi-platonic and wholly unprofitable flirtation with him. During this epoch she wore out the remnant of her summer clothes and laid in substitutes; rather encouraged than otherwise by the fact that she had long since lost touch with the amount of her balance at the bank.

3. An expiatory and age-long sojourn of three weeks with relatives at an Essex vicarage, mitigated only by persistent bicycling with her uncle's curate. The result, as might have been predicted by any one acquainted with Miss Fitzroy, was that the curate's affections were diverted from the bourne long appointed for them, namely, the eldest daughter of the house, and that Fanny departed in blackest disgrace, with the single consolation of knowing that she would never be asked to the vicarage again.

Finally she returned, third-class, to her home in Ireland, with nothing to show for the expedition except a new and very smart habit, and a vague assurance that Captain Carteret would give her a mount now and then with Freddy Alexander's hounds. Captain Carteret was to be on detachment at Enniscar.

PART II

Mr. William Fennessy, lately returned from America, at present publican in Enniscar and proprietor of a small farm on its outskirts, had taken a grey mare to the forge.

It was now November, and the mare had been out at grass for nearly three months, somewhat to the detriment of her figure, but very much to her general advantage. Even in the south-west of Ireland it is not usual to keep horses out quite so late in the year, but Mr. Fennessy, having begun his varied career as a travelling tinker, was not the man to be bound by convention. He had provided the mare with the society of a donkey and two sheep, and with the shelter of a filthy and ruinous cowshed. Taking into consideration the fact that he had only paid seven pounds ten shillings for her, he thought this accommodation was as much as she was entitled to.

She was now drooping and dozing in a dark corner of the forge, waiting her turn to be shod, while the broken spring of a car was being patched, as shaggy and as dirty a creature as had ever stood there.

"Where did you get that one?" inquired the owner of the car of Mr. Fennessy, in the course of much lengthy conversation.

"I got her from a cousin of my own that died down in the County Limerick," said Mr. Fennessy in his most agreeable manner. "'Twas himself bred her, and she was near deshtroyed fallin' back on a harra' with him. It's for postin' I have her."

"She's shlack enough yet," said the carman.

"Ah, wait awhile!" said Mr. Fennessy easily, "in a week's time when I'll have her clipped out, she'll be as clean as amber."

The conversation flowed on to other themes.

It was nearly dark when the carman took his departure, and the smith, a silent youth with sore eyes, caught hold of one of the grey mare's fetlocks and told her to "lift!" He examined each hoof in succession by the light of a candle stuck in a bottle, raked his fire together, and then, turning to Mr. Fennessy, remarked:--

"Ye'd laugh if ye were here the day I put a slipper on this one, an' she afther comin' out o' the thrain--last June it was. 'Twas one Connolly back from Craffroe side was taking her from the station; him that thrained her for Miss Fitzroy. She gave him the two heels in the face." The glow from the fire illumined the smith's sardonic grin of remembrance. "She had a sandcrack in the near fore that time, and there's the sign of it yet."

The Cinderella-like episode of the slipper had naturally not entered into Mr. Fennessy's calculations, but he took the unforeseen without a change of countenance.

"Well, now," he said deliberately, "I was sayin' to meself on the road a while ago, if there was one this side o' the counthry would know her it'd be yerself."

The smith took the compliment with a blink of his sore eyes.

"Annyone'd be hard set to know her now," he said.

There was a pause, during which a leap of sparks answered each thump of the hammer on the white hot iron, and Mr. Fennessy arranged his course of action.

"Well, Larry," he said, "I'll tell ye now what no one in this counthry knows but meself and Patsey Crimmeen. Sure I know it's as good to tell a thing to the ground as to tell it to yerself!"

He lowered his voice.

"'Twas Mr. Gunning of Streamstown bought that one from Miss Fitzroy at the Dublin Show, and a hundhred pound he gave for her!"

The smith mentally docked this sum by seventy pounds, but said, "By dam!" in polite convention.

"'Twasn't a week afther that I got her for twenty-five pounds!"

The smith made a further mental deduction equally justified by the facts; the long snore and wheeze of the bellows filled the silence, and the dirty walls flushed and glowed with the steady crescendo and diminuendo of the glow.

The ex-tinker picked up the bottle with the candle. "Look at that!" he said, lowering the light and displaying a long transverse scar beginning at the mare's knee and ending in an enlarged fetlock.

"I seen that," said the smith.

"And look at that!" continued Mr. Fennessy, putting back the shaggy hair on her shoulder. A wide and shiny patch of black skin showed where the hatter's plate glass had flayed the shoulder. "She played the divil goin' through the streets, and made flitthers of herself this way, in a shop window. Gunning give the word to shoot her. The dealer's boy told Patsey Crimmeen. 'Twas Patsey was caring her at the show for Miss Fitzroy. Shtan' will ye!"--this to the mare, whose eyes glinted white as she flung away her head from the light of the candle.

"Whatever fright she got she didn't forget it," said the smith.

"I was up in Dublin meself the same time," pursued Mr. Fennessy. "Afther I seem' Patsey I took a sthroll down to Brennan's yard. The leg was in two halves, barrin' the shkin, and the showldher swoll up as big as a sack o' meal. I was three or four days goin' down to look at her this way, and I seen she wasn't as bad as what they thought. I come in one morning, and the boy says to me, 'The boss has three horses comin' in to-day, an' I dunno where'll we put this one.' I goes to Brennan, and he sitting down to his breakfast, and the wife with him. 'Sir,' says I, 'for the honour of God sell me that mare!' We had hard strugglin' then. In the latther end the wife says, 'It's as good for ye to part her, James,' says she, 'and Mr. Gunning'll never know what way she went. This honest man'll never say where he got her.' 'I will not, ma'am,' says I. 'I have a brother in the postin' line in Belfast, and it's for him I'm buyin' her.'"

The, process of making nail-holes in the shoe seemed to engross the taciturn young smith's attention for the next minute or two.

"There was a man over from Craffroe in town yesterday," he observed presently, "that said Mr. Gunning was lookin' out for a cob, and he'd fancy one that would lep."

He eyed his work sedulously as he spoke.

Something, it might have been the light of the candle, woke a flicker in Mr. Fennessy's eye. He passed his hand gently down the mare's quarter.

"Supposing now that the mane was off her, and something about six inches of a dock took off her tail, what sort of a cob d'ye think she'd make, Larry?"

The smith, with a sudden falsetto cackle of laughter, plunged the shoe into a tub of water, in which it gurgled and spluttered as if in appreciation of the jest.

PART III

Dotted at intervals throughout society are the people endowed with the faculty for "getting up things". They are dauntless people, filled with the power of driving lesser and deeper reluctant spirits before them; remorseless to the timid, carneying to the stubborn.

Of such was Mrs. Carteret, with powers matured in hill-stations in India, mellowed by much voyaging in P. and O. steamers. Not even an environment as unpromising as that of Enniscar in its winter torpor had power to dismay her. A public whose artistic tastes had hitherto been nourished upon travelling circuses, Nationalist meetings, and missionary magic lanterns in the Wesleyan schoolhouse, was, she argued, practically virgin soil, and would ecstatically respond to any form of cultivation.

"I know there's not much talent to be had," she said combatively to her husband, "but we'll just black our faces, and call ourselves the Green Coons or something, and it will be all right!"

"Dashed if I'll black my face again," said Captain Carteret; "I call it rot trying to get up anything here. There's no one to do anything."

"Well, there's ourselves and little Taylour" ("little Taylour," it may be explained, was Captain Carteret's subaltern), "that's two banjoes and a bones anyhow; and Freddy Alexander, and there's your dear friend Fanny Fitz--she'll be home in a few days, and these two big Hamilton girls--"

"Oh, Lord!" ejaculated Captain Carteret.

"Oh, yes!" continued Mrs. Carteret, unheedingly, "and there's Mr. Gunning; he'll come if Fanny Fitz does."

"He'll not be much advantage when he does come," said Captain Carteret spitefully.

"Oh, he sings," said Mrs. Carteret, arranging her neat small fringe at the glass--"rather a good voice. You needn't be afraid, my dear, I'll arrange that the fascinating Fanny shall sit next you!"

Upon this somewhat unstable basis the formation of the troupe of Green Coons was undertaken. Mrs. Carteret took off her coat to the work, or rather, to be accurate, she put on a fur-lined one, and attended a Nationalist meeting in the Town Hall to judge for herself how the voices carried. She returned rejoicing--she had sat at the back of the hall, and had not lost a syllable of the oratory, even during sundry heated episodes, discreetly summarised by the local paper as "interruption". The Town Hall was chartered, superficially cleansed, and in the space of a week the posters had gone forth.

By what means it was accomplished that Rupert Gunning should attend the first rehearsal he did not exactly understand; he found himself enmeshed in a promise to meet every one else at the Town Hall with tea at the Carterets' afterwards. Up to this point the fact that he was to appear before the public with a blackened face had been diplomatically withheld from him, and an equal diplomacy was shown on his arrival in the deputing of Miss Fitzroy to break the news to him.

"Mrs. Carteret says it's really awfully becoming," said Fanny, breathless and brilliant from assiduous practice of a hornpipe under Captain Carteret's tuition, "and as for trouble! We might as well make a virtue of necessity in this incredibly dirty place; my hands are black already, and I've only swept the stage!"

She was standing at the edge of the platform that was to serve as the stage, looking down at him, and it may be taken as a sufficient guide to his mental condition that his abhorrence of the prospect for himself was swallowed up by fury at the thought of it for her.

"Are you--do you mean to tell me you are going to dance **with a black face**?" he demanded in bitter and incongruous wrath.

"No, I'm going to dance with Captain Carteret!" replied Fanny frivolously, "and so can you if you like!"

She was maddeningly pretty as she smiled down at him, with her bright hair roughened, and the afterglow of the dance alight in her eyes and cheeks. Nevertheless, for one whirling moment, the old Adam, an Adam blissfully unaware of the existence of Eve, asserted himself in Rupert. He picked up his cap and stick without a word, and turned towards the door. There, however, he was confronted by Mrs. Carteret, tugging at a line of chairs attached to a plank, like a very small bird with a very large twig. To refuse the aid that she immediately demanded was impossible, and even before the future back row of the sixpennies had been towed to its moorings, he realised that hateful as it would be to stay and join in these distasteful revels, it would be better than going home and thinking about them.

From this the intelligent observer may gather that absence had had its traditional, but by no means invariable, effect upon the heart of Mr. Gunning, and, had any further stimulant been needed, it had been supplied in the last few minutes by the aggressive and possessive manner of Captain Carteret.

The rehearsal progressed after the manner of amateur rehearsals. The troupe, with the exception of Mr. Gunning, who remained wrapped in silence, talked irrepressibly, and quite inappropriately to their role as Green Coons. Freddy Alexander and Mr. Taylour bear-fought untiringly for possession of the bones and the position of Corner Man; Mrs. Carteret alone had a copy of the music that was to be practised, and in consequence, the company hung heavily over her at the piano in a deafening and discordant swarm. The two tall Hamiltons, hitherto speechless by nature and by practice, became suddenly exhilarated at finding themselves in the inner circle of the soldiery, and bubbled with impotent suggestions and reverential laughter at the witticisms of Mr. Taylour. Fanny Fitz and Captain Carteret finally removed themselves to a grimy corner behind the proscenium, and there practised, **sotto voce**, the song with banjo accompaniment that was to culminate in the hornpipe. Freddy Alexander had gone forth to purchase a pack of cards, in the futile hope that he could prevail upon Mrs. Carteret to allow him to inflict conjuring tricks upon the audience.

"As if there were anything on earth that bored people as much as card tricks!" said that experienced lady to Rupert Gunning. "Look here, **would** you mind reading over these riddles, to see which you'd like to have to answer. Now, here's a local one. I'll ask it--'Why am dis room like de Enniscar Demesne?'--and then **you'll** say, 'Because dere am so many pretty little deers in it'!"

"Oh, I couldn't possibly do that!" said Rupert hastily, alarmed as well as indignant; "I'm afraid I really must go now--"

He had to pass by Fanny Fitz on his way out of the hall. There was something vexed and forlorn about him, and, being sympathetic, she perceived it, though not its cause.

"You're deserting us!" she said, looking up at him.

"I have an appointment," he said stiffly, his glance evading hers, and resting on

Captain Carteret's well-clipped little black head.

Some of Fanny's worst scrapes had been brought about by her incapacity to allow any one to part from her on bad terms, and, moreover, she liked Rupert Gunning. She cast about in her mind for something conciliatory to say to him.

"When are you going to show me the cob that you bought at the Horse Show?"

The olive branch thus confidently tendered had a somewhat withering reception.

"The cob I bought at the Horse Show?" Mr. Gunning repeated with an increase of rigidity, "Oh, yes--I got rid of it."

He paused; the twanging of Captain Carteret's banjo bridged the interval imperturbably.

"Why had you to get rid of it?" asked Fanny, still sympathetic.

"She was a failure!" said Rupert vindictively; "I made a fool of myself in buying her!"

Fanny looked at him sideways from under her lashes.

"And I had counted on your giving me a mount on her now and then!"

Rupert forgot his wrath, forgot even the twanging banjo.

"I've just got another cob," he said quickly; "she jumps very well, and if you'd like to hunt her next Tuesday--"

"Oh, thanks awfully, but Captain Carteret has promised me a mount for next Tuesday!" said the perfidious Fanny.

Mrs. Carteret, on her knees by a refractory footlight, watched with anxiety Mr. Gunning's abrupt departure from the room.

"Fanny!" she said severely, "what have you been doing to that man?"

"Oh, nothing!" said Fanny.

"If you've put him off singing I'll never forgive you!" continued Mrs. Carteret, advancing on her knees to the next footlight.

"I tell you I've done nothing to him," said Fanny Fitz guiltily.

"Give me the hammer!" said Mrs. Carteret. "Have I eyes, or have I not?"

"He's awfully keen about her!" Mrs. Carteret said that evening to her husband. "Bad temper is one of the worst signs. Men in love are always cross."

"Oh, he's a rotter!" said Captain Carteret conclusively.

In the meantime the object of this condemnation was driving his ten Irish miles home, by the light of a frosty full moon. Between the shafts of his cart a trim-looking mare of about fifteen hands trotted lazily, forging, shying, and generally comporting herself in a way only possible to a grass-fed animal who has been in the hands of such as Mr. William Fennessy. The thick and dingy mane that had hung impartially on each side of her neck, now, together with the major portion of her voluminous tail, adorned the manure heap in the rear of the Fennessy public-house. The pallid fleece in which she had been muffled had given place to a polished coat of iron-grey, that looked black in the moonlight. A week of over-abundant oats had made her opinionated, but had not, so far, restored to her the fine lady nervousness that had landed her in the window of the hat shop.

Rupert laid the whip along her fat sides with bitter disfavour. She was a brute in harness, he said to himself, her blemished fetlock was uglier than he had at first thought, and even though she had yesterday schooled over two miles of country like an old stager, she was too small to carry him, and she was not, apparently, wanted to carry any one else. Here the purchase received a very disagreeable cut on the neck that interrupted her speculations as to the nature of the shadows of telegraph-posts. To have bought two useless horses in four months was pretty average bad luck. It was also pretty bad luck to have been born a fool. Reflection here became merged in the shapeless and futile fumings of a man badly in love and preposterously jealous.

Known only to the elect among entertainment promoters are the methods employed by Mrs. Carteret to float the company of The Green Coons. The fact remains that on the appointed night the chosen troupe, approximately word-perfect, and with spirits something chastened by stage fright, were assembled in the clerk's room of the Enniscar Town Hall, round a large basin filled horribly with a compound of burnt cork and water.

"It's not as bad as it looks!" said Mrs. Carteret, plunging in her hands and heroically smearing her face with a mass of black oozy matter believed to be a sponge. "It's quite becoming if you do it thoroughly. Mind, all of you, get it well into your ears and the roots of your hair!"

The Hamiltons, giggling wildly, submitted themselves to the ministrations of Freddy Alexander, and Mrs. Carteret, appallingly transformed into a little West Indian coolie woman, applied the sponge to the shrinking Fanny Fitz.

"Will you do Mr. Gunning, Fanny?" she whispered into one of the ears that she had conscientiously blackened. "I think he'd bear it better from you!"

"I shall do nothing of the kind!" replied Fanny, with a dignity somewhat impaired by her ebon countenance and monstrous green turban.

"Why not?"

Mrs. Carteret's small neat features seemed unnaturally sharpened, and her eyes and teeth glittered in her excitement.

"For goodness' sake, take your awful little black face away, Mabel!" exclaimed Fanny hysterically. "It quite frightens me! I'm **very** angry with Mr. Gunning! I'll tell you why some other time."

"Well, don't forget you've got to say 'Buck up, Sambo!' to him after he's sung his song, and you may fight with him as much as you like afterwards," said Mrs. Carteret, hurrying off to paint glaring vermilion mouths upon the loudly protesting Hamiltons.

During these vicissitudes, Rupert Gunning, arrayed in a green swallow-tailed calico coat, short white cotton trousers, and a skimpy nigger wig, presented a pitiful example of the humiliations which the allied forces of love and jealousy can bring upon the just. Fanny Fitz has since admitted that, in spite of the wrath that burned within her, the sight of Mr. Gunning morosely dabbing his long nose with the repulsive sponge that was shared by the troupe, almost moved her to compassion.

A pleasing impatience was already betraying itself in cat-calls and stampings from the sixpenny places, and Mrs. Carteret, flitting like a sheep dog round her flock, arranged them in couples and drove them before her on to the stage, singing in chorus, with a fair assumption of hilarity, "As we go marching through Georgia".

For Fanny Fitz the subsequent proceedings became merged in a nightmare of blinding heat and glare, made actual only by poignant anxiety as to the length of her green skirt. The hope that she might be unrecognisable was shattered by the yell of "More power, Miss Fanny!" that crested the thunderous encore evoked by her hornpipe with Captain Carteret, and the question of the skirt was decided by the fact that her aunts, in the front row, firmly perused their programmes from the beginning of her dance to its conclusion.

The entertainment went with varying success after the manner of its kind.

The local hits and personal allusions, toilfully compiled and ardently believed in, were received in damping silence, while Rupert Gunning's song, of the truculent order dedicated to basses, and sung by him with a face that would have done credit to Othello, received an ovation that confirmed Captain Carteret in his contempt for country audiences. The performance raged to its close in a "Cake Walk," to the inspiring strains of "Razors a-flying through the air," and the curtain fell on what the Enniscar *Independent* described cryptically as "a ***tout ensemble a la conversazione*** that was refreshingly unique".

"Five minutes more and I should have had heat apoplexy!" said Mrs. Carteret, hurling her turban across the clerk's room, "but it all went splendidly! Empty that basin out of the window, somebody, and give me the vaseline. The last time I blacked my face it was covered with red spots for a week afterwards because I used soap instead of vaseline!"

Rupert Gunning approached Fanny with an open note in his hand.

"I've had this from your aunt," he said, handing it to her; it was decorated with sooty thumb marks, to which Fanny's black claw contributed a fresh batch as she took it, but she read it without a smile.

It was to the effect that the heat of the room had been too much for the elder Misses Fitzroy, and they had therefore gone home, but as Mr. Gunning had to pass their gate perhaps he would be kind enough to drive their niece home.

"Oh--" said Fanny, in tones from which dismay was by no means eliminated. "How stupid of Aunt Rachel!"

"I'm afraid there seems no way out of it for you," said Rupert offendedly.

A glimpse of their two wrathful black faces in the glass abruptly checked Fanny's desire to say something crushing. At this juncture she would rather have died than laughed.

Burnt cork is not lightly to be removed at the first essay, and when, half an hour later, Fanny Fitz, with a pale and dirty face, stood under the dismal light of the lamp outside the Town Hall, waiting for Mr. Gunning's trap, she had the pleasure of hearing a woman among the loiterers say compassionately:--

"God help her, the crayture! She looks like a servant that'd be bate out with work!"

Mr. Gunning's new cob stood hearkening with flickering ears to the various commotions of the street--she understood them all perfectly well, but her soul being unlifted by reason of oats, she chose to resent them as impertinences. Having tolerated with difficulty the instalment of Miss Fitzroy in the trap, she started with a flourish, and pulled hard until clear of the town and its flaring public-houses. On the open road, with nothing more enlivening than the dark hills, half-seen in the light of the rising moon, she settled down. Rupert turned to his silent companion. He had become aware during the evening that something was wrong, and his own sense of injury was frightened into the background.

"What do you think of my new buy?" he said pacifically, "she's a good goer, isn't she?"

"Very," replied Fanny.

Silence again reigned. One or two further attempts at conversation met with equal discouragement. The miles passed by. At length, as the mare slackened to walk up a long hill, Rupert said with a voice that had the shake of pent-up injury:--

"I've been wondering what I've done to be put into Coventry like this!"

"I thought you probably wouldn't care to speak to me!" was Fanny's astonishing reply, delivered in tones of ice.

"I!" he stammered, "not care to speak to *you*! You ought to know--"

"Yes, indeed, I do know!" broke in Fanny, passing from the frigid to the torrid zone with characteristic speed, "I know what a *failure* your horse-dealing at the Dublin Show was! I've heard how you bought my mare, and had her shot the same night, because you wouldn't take the trouble even to go and look at her after the poor little thing was hurt! Oh! I can't bear even to *think* of it!"

Rupert Gunning remained abjectly and dumfoundedly silent.

"And then," continued Fanny, whirling on to the final point of her indictment, "you pretended to Captain Carteret and me that the horse you had bought was 'a common brute,' *a cob for carting*, and you said the other night that you had made a fool of yourself over it! I didn't know then all about it, but I do now. Captain Carteret heard about it from the dealer in Dublin. Even the dealer said it was a pity you hadn't given the mare a chance!"

"It's all perfectly true," said Rupert, in a low voice.

A soft answer, so far from turning away wrath, frequently inflames it.

"Then I think there's no more to be said!" said Fanny hotly.

There was silence. They had reached the top of the hill, and the grey mare began to trot.

"Well, there's just one thing I should like to say," said Rupert awkwardly, his breath coming very short, "I couldn't help everything going wrong about the mare. It was just my bad luck. I only bought her to please you. They told me she couldn't get right after the accident. What was the good of my going to look at her? I wanted to cross in the boat with you. Whatever I did I did for you. I would do anything in the world for you--"

It was at this crucial moment that there arose suddenly from the dim grey road in front of them a slightly greyer shadow, a shadow that limped amid the clanking of chains. The Connemara mare, now masquerading as a County Cork cob, asked for nothing better. If it were a ghost, she was legitimately entitled to flee from it; if, as was indeed the case, it was a donkey, she made a point of shying at donkeys. She realised that, by a singular stroke of good fortune, the reins were lying in loops on her back.

A snort, a sideways bound, a couple of gleeful kicks on the dashboard, and she was away at full gallop, with one rein under her tail, and a pleasant open road before her.

"It's all right!" said Rupert, recovering his balance by a hair-breadth, and feeling in his heart that it was all wrong, "the Craffroe Hill will stop her. Hold on to the rail."

Fanny said nothing. It was, indeed, all that she could do to keep her seat in the trap, with which the rushing road was playing cup and ball; she was, besides, not one of the people who are conversational in emergencies. When an animal, as active and artful as the Connemara mare, is going at some twenty miles an hour, with one of the reins under its tail, endeavours to detach the rein are not much avail, and when the tail is still tender from recent docking, they are a good deal worse than useless. Having twice nearly fallen on his head, Rupert abandoned the attempt and prayed for the long stiff ascent of the Craffroe Hill.

It came swiftly out of the grey moonlight. At its foot another road forked to the right; instead of facing the hill that led to home and stable, the mare swung into the side road, with one wheel up on the grass, and the cushions slipping from the seat, and Rupert, just saving the situation with the left rein that remained to him, said to himself that they were in for a bad business.

For a mile they swung and clattered along it, with the wind striking and splitting against their faces like a cold and tearing stream of water; a light wavered and disappeared across the pallid fields to the left, a group of starveling trees on a hill slid up into the skyline behind them, and at last it seemed as if some touch of self-control, some suggestion of having had enough of the joke, was shortening the mare's grasping stride. The trap pitched more than ever as she came up into the shafts and back into her harness; she twisted suddenly to the left into a narrow lane, cleared the corner by an impossible fluke, and Fanny Fitz was hurled ignominiously on to Rupert Gunning's lap. Long briars and twigs struck them from either side, the trap bumped in craggy ruts and slashed through wide puddles, then reeled irretrievably over a heap of stones and tilted against the low bank to the right.

Without any exact knowledge of how she got there, Fanny found herself on her hands and knees in a clump of bracken on top of the bank; Rupert was already picking himself out of rugs and other jetsam in the field below her, and the mare was proceeding up the lane at a disorderly trot, having jerked the trap on to its legs again from its reclining position.

Fanny was lifted down into the lane; she told him that she was not hurt, but her knees shook, her hands trembled, and the arm that was round her tightened its clasp in silence. When a man is strongly moved by tenderness and anxiety and relief, he can say little to make it known; he need not--it is known beyond all telling by the one other person whom it concerns. She felt suddenly that she was safe, that his heart was torn for her sake, and that the tension of the last ten minutes had been great. It went through her with a pang, and her head swayed against his arm. In a moment she felt his lips on her hair, on her temple, and the oldest, the most familiar of all words of endearment was spoken at her ear. She recovered herself, but in a new world. She tried to walk on up the lane, but stumbled in the deep ruts and found the supporting arm again ready at need. She did not resist it.

A shrill neigh arose in front of them. The mare had pulled up at a closed gate, and was apparently apostrophising some low farm buildings beyond it. A dog barked hysterically, the door of a cowshed burst open, and a man came out with a lantern.

"Oh, I know now where we are!" cried Fanny wildly, "it's Johnny Connolly's!

Oh, Johnny, Johnny Connolly, we've been run away with!"

"For God's sake!" responded Johnny Connolly, standing stock still in his amazement, "is that Miss Fanny?"

"Get hold of the mare," shouted Rupert, "or she'll jump the gate!"

Johnny Connolly advanced, still calling upon his God, and the mare uttered a low but vehement neigh.

"Ye're deshtroyed, Miss Fanny! And Mr. Gunning, the Lord save us! Ye're killed the two o' ye! What happened ye at all? Woa, gerr'l, woa, gerrlie! Ye'd say she knew me, the crayture."

The mare was rubbing her dripping face and neck against the farmer's shoulder, with hoarse whispering snorts of recognition and pleasure. He held his lantern high to look at her.

"Musha, why wouldn't she know me!" he roared, "sure it's yer own mare, Miss Fanny! 'Tis the Connemara mare I thrained for ye! And may the divil sweep and roast thim that has it told through all the counthry that she was killed!"

A GRAND FILLY

I am an Englishman. I say this without either truculence or vainglorying, rather with humility--a mere Englishman, who submits his Plain Tale from the Western Hills with the conviction that the Kelt who may read it will think him more mere than ever.

I was in Yorkshire last season when what is trivially called "the cold snap" came upon us. I had five horses eating themselves silly all the time, and I am not going to speak of it. I don't consider it a subject to be treated lightly. It was in about the thickest of it that I heard from a man I know in Ireland. He is a little old horse-coping sportsman with a red face and iron-grey whiskers, who has kept hounds all his life; or, rather, he has always had hounds about, on much the same conditions that other men have rats. The rats are indubitably there, and feed themselves variously, and so do old Robert Trinder's "Rioters," which is their **nom de guerre** in the County Corkerry (the few who know anything of the map of Ireland may possibly identify the two counties buried in this cryptogram).

I meet old Robert most years at the Dublin Horse Show, and every now and then he has sold me a pretty good horse, so when he wrote and renewed a standing invitation, assuring me that there was open weather, and that he had a grand four-year-old filly to sell, I took him at his word, and started at once. The journey lasted for twenty-eight hours, going hard all the time, and during the last three of them there were no foot-warmers and the cushions became like stones enveloped in mustard plasters. Old Trinder had not sent to the station for me, and it was pelting rain, so I had to drive seven miles in a thing that only exists south of the Limerick Junction, and is called a "jingle". A jingle is a square box of painted canvas with no back to it, because, as was luminously explained to me, you must have some way to get into it, and I had to sit sideways in it, with my portmanteau bucking like a three-year-old on the seat opposite to me. It fell out on the road twice going uphill. After the second fall my hair tonic slowly oozed forth from the seams, and added a fresh ingredient to the smells of the grimy cushions and the damp hay that furnished the machine. My hair tonic costs eight-and-sixpence a bottle.

There is probably not in the United Kingdom a worse-planned entrance gate than Robert Trinder's. You come at it obliquely on the side of a crooked hill, squeeze between its low pillars with an inch to spare each side, and immediately drop down a yet steeper hill, which lasts for the best part of a quarter of a mile. The jingle went swooping and jerking down into the unknown, till, through the portholes on either side of the driver's legs, I saw Lisangle House. It had looked decidedly better in large red letters at the top of old Robert's notepaper than it did at the top of his lawn, being no more than a square yellow box of a house, that had been made a fool of by being promiscuously trimmed with battlements. Just as my jingle tilted me in backwards against the flight of steps, I heard through the open door a loud and piercing yell; following on it came the thunder of many feet, and the next instant a hound bolted down the steps with a large plucked turkey in its mouth. Close in its wake fled a brace of puppies, and behind them, variously armed, pursued what appeared to be the staff of Lisangle House. They went past me in full cry, leaving a general impression of dirty aprons, flying hair, and onions, and I feel sure that there were bare feet somewhere in it. My carman leaped from his perch and joined in the chase, and the whole party swept from my astonished gaze round or into a clump of bushes. At this juncture I was not sorry to hear Robert Trinder's voice greeting me as if nothing unusual were occurring.

"Upon me honour, it's the Captain! You're welcome, sir, you're welcome! Come in, come in, don't mind the horse at all; he'll eat the grass there as he's done many a time before! When the gerr'ls have old Amazon cot they'll bring in your things."

(Perhaps I ought to mention at once that Mr. Trinder belongs to the class who are known in Ireland as "Half-sirs". You couldn't say he was a gentleman, and he himself wouldn't have tried to say so. But, as a matter of fact, I have seen worse imitations.)

Robert was delighted to see me, and I had had a whisky-and-soda and been shown two or three more hound puppies before it occurred to him to introduce me to his aunt. I had not expected an aunt, as Robert is well on the heavenward side of sixty; but there she was: she made me think of a badly preserved Egyptian mummy with a brogue. I am always a little afraid of my hostess, but there was something about Robert's aunt that made me know I was a worm. She came down to dinner in a bonnet and black kid gloves--a circumstance that alone was awe-inspiring. She sat entrenched at the head of the table behind an enormous dish of thickly jacketed potatoes, and, though she scorned to speak to Robert or me, she kept up a sort of whispered wrangle with the parlour-maid all the time. The latter's red hair hung down over her shoulders--and at intervals over mine also--in horrible luxuriance, and recalled the leading figure in the pursuit of Amazon; there was, moreover, something about the heavy boots in which she tramped round the table that suggested that Amazon had sought sanctuary in the cow-house. I have done some roughing it in my time, and I am not over-particular, but I admit that it was rather a shock to meet the turkey itself again, more especially as it was the sole item of the *menu*. There was no doubt of its identity, as it was short of a leg, and half the breast had been shaved away. The aunt must have read my thoughts in my face. She fixed her small implacable eyes on mine for one quelling instant, then she looked at Robert. Her nephew was obviously afraid to meet her eye; he coughed uneasily, and handed a surreptitious potato to the puppy who was sitting under his chair.

"This place is rotten with dogs," said the aunt; with which announcement she retired from the conversation, and fell again to the slaughter of the parlour-maid. I timidly ate my portion of turkey and tried not to think about the cow-house.

It rained all night. I could hear the water hammering into something that rang like a gong; and each time I rolled over in the musty trough of my feather-bed I fractiously asked myself why the mischief they had left the tap running all night. Next morning the matter was explained when, on demanding a bath, I was told that "there wasn't but one in the house, and 'twas undher the rain-down. But sure ye can have it," with which it was dragged in full of dirty water and flakes of whitewash, and when I got out of it I felt as if I had been through the Bankruptcy Court.

The day was windy and misty--a combination of weather possible only in Ireland--but there was no snow, and Robert Trinder, seated at breakfast in a purple-red hunting coat, dingy drab breeches, and woollen socks, assured me that it was turning out a grand morning.

I distinctly liked the looks of my mount when Jerry the Whip pulled her out of the stable for me. She was big and brown, with hindquarters that looked like jumping; she was also very dirty and obviously underfed. None the less she was lively enough, and justified Jerry's prediction that "she'd be apt to shake a couple or three bucks out of herself when she'd see the hounds". Old Robert was on an ugly brute of a yellow horse, rather like a big mule, who began the day by bucking out of the yard gate as if he had been trained by Buffalo Bill. It was at this juncture that I first really respected Robert Trinder; his retention of his seat was so unstudied, and his command of appropriate epithets so complete.

Jerry and the hounds awaited us on the road, the latter as mixed a party as I have ever come across. There were about fourteen couple in all, and they ranged in style from a short-legged black-and-tan harrier, who had undoubtedly had an uncle who was a dachshund, to a thing with a head like a greyhound, a snow-white body, and a feathered stern that would have been a credit to a setter. In between these extremes came several broken-haired Welshmen, some dilapidated 24-inch foxhounds, and a lot of pale-coloured hounds, whose general effect was that of the tablecloth on which we had eaten our breakfast that morning, being dirty white, covered with stains that looked like either tea or egg, or both.

"Them's the old Irish breed," said Robert, as the yellow horse voluntarily stopped short to avoid stepping on one of them; "there's no better. That Gaylass there would take a line up Patrick Street on a fair day, and you'd live and die seeing her kill rats."

I am bound to say I thought it more likely that I should live to see her and some of her relations killing sheep, judging by their manners along the road; but we got to Letter cross-roads at last with no more than an old hen and a wandering cur dog on our collective consciences. The road and its adjacent fences were thronged with foot people, mostly strapping young men and boys, in the white flannel coats and slouched felt hats that strike a stranger with their unusualness and picturesqueness.

"Do you ever have a row with Land Leaguers?" I asked, noting their sticks, while the warnings of a sentimental Radical friend as to the danger of encountering an infuriated Irish peasantry suddenly assumed plausibility.

"Land League? The dear help ye! Who'd be bothered with the Land League here?" said Robert, shoving the yellow horse into the crowd; "let the hounds through, boys, can't ye? No, Captain, but 'tis Saint November's Day, as they call it, a great holiday, and there isn't a ruffian in the country but has come out with his blagyard dog to head the fox!"

A grin of guilt passed over the faces of the audience.

"There's plinty foxes in the hill, Mr. Thrinder," shouted one of them; "Dan Murphy says there isn't a morning but he'd see six or eight o' them hoppin' there."

"Faith, 'tis thrue for you," corroborated Dan Murphy. "If ye had thim gethered in a quarther of ground and dhropped a pin from th' elements, 'twould reach one o' thim!"

(As a matter of fact, I haven't a notion what Mr. Murphy meant, but that is what he said, so I faithfully record it.)

The riders were farmers and men of Robert's own undetermined class, and there was hardly a horse out who was more than four years old, saving two or three who were nineteen. Robert pushed through them and turned up a bohireen-- *i.e.*, a narrow and incredibly badly made lane--and I presently heard him cheering the hounds into covert. As to that covert, imagine a hill that in any civilised country would be called a mountain: its nearer side a cliff, with just enough slope to give root-hold to giant furze bushes, its summit a series of rocky and boggy terraces, trending down at one end into a ravine, and at the other becoming merged in the depths of an aboriginal wood of low scrubby oak trees. It seemed as feasible to ride a horse over it as over the roof of York Minster. I hadn't the vaguest idea what to do or where to go, and I clave to Jerry the Whip.

The hounds were scrambling like monkeys along the side of the hill; so were the country boys with their curs; old Trinder moved parallel with them along its base. Jerry galloped away to the ravine, and there dismounting, struggled up by zig-zag cattle paths to the comparative levels of the summit. I did the same, and was pretty well blown by the time I got to the top, as the filly scorned the zigzags, and hauled me up as straight as she could go over the rocks and furze bushes. A few other fellows had followed us, and we all pursued on along the top of the hill.

Suddenly Jerry stopped short and held up his hand. A hound spoke below us, then another, and then came a halloa from Jerry that made the filly quiver all over. The fox had come up over the low fence that edged the cliff, and was running along the terrace in front of us. Old Robert below us--I could almost have chucked a stone on to him--gave an answering screech, and one by one the hounds fought their way up over the fence and went away on the line, throwing their tongues in a style that did one good to hear. Our only way ahead lay along a species of trench between the hill, on whose steep side we were standing, and the cliff fence. Jerry kicked the spurs into his good ugly little horse, and making him jump down into the trench, squeezed along it after the hounds. But the delay of waiting for them had got the filly's temper up. When I faced her at the trench she reared, and whirled round, and pranced backwards in, considering the circumstances, a highly discomposing way. The rest of the field crowded through the furze past me and down into the trench, and twice I thought the mare would land herself and me on top of one of them. I don't wonder she was frightened. I know I was. There was nothing between us and a hundred-foot drop but this narrow trench and a low, rotten fence, and the fool behaved as though she wanted to jump it all. I hope no one will ever erect an equestrian statue in my honour; now that I have experienced the sensation of ramping over nothing, I find I dislike it. I believe I might have been there now, but just then a couple of hounds came up, and before I knew what she was at, the filly had jumped down after them into the trench as if she had been doing it all her life. I was not long about picking the others up; the filly could gallop anyhow, and we thundered on over ground where, had I been on foot, I should have liked a guide and an alpenstock. At intervals we jumped things made of sharp stones, and slates, and mud; I don't know whether they were banks or walls. Sometimes the horses changed feet on them, sometimes they flew the whole affair, according to their individual judgment. Sometimes we were splashing over sedgy patches that looked and felt like buttered toast, sometimes floundering through stuff resembling an ill-made chocolate souffle, whether intended for a ploughed field or a partially drained bog-hole I could not determine, and all was fenced as carefully as cricket-pitches. Presently the hounds took a swing to the left and over the edge of the hill again, and our leader Jerry turned sharp off after them, down a track that seemed to have been dug out of the face of the hill. I should have liked to get off and lead, but they did not give me time, and we suddenly found ourselves joined to Robert Trinder and his company of infantry, all going hard for the oak wood that I mentioned before.

It was pretty to see the yellow horse jump. Nothing came amiss to him, and he didn't seem able to make a mistake. There was a stone stile out of a bohireen that stopped every one, and he changed feet on the flag on top and went down by the steps on the other side. No one need believe this unless they like, but I saw him do it. The country boys were most exhilarating. How they got there I don't know, but they seemed to spring up before us wherever we went. They cheered every jump, they pulled away the astounding obstacles that served as gates (such as the end of an iron bedstead, a broken harrow, or a couple of cartwheels), and their power of seeing the fox through a stone wall or a hill could only be equalled by the Roentgen rays. We fought our way through the oak wood, and out over a boggy bounds ditch into open country at last. The Rioters had come out of the wood on a screaming scent, and big and little were running together in a compact body, followed, like the tail of a kite, by a string of yapping country curs. The country was all grass, enchantingly green and springy; the jumps were big, yet not too big, and there were no two alike; the filly pulled hard, but not too hard, and she was jumping like a deer; I felt that all I had heard of Irish hunting had not been overstated.

We had been running for half an hour when we checked at a farmhouse; the yellow horse had been leading the hunt all the time, making a noise like a steam-engine, but perfectly undefeated, and our numbers were reduced to five. An old woman and a girl rushed out of the yard to meet us, screaming like sea-gulls.

"He's gone south this five minutes! I was out spreadin' clothes, and I seen him circling round the Kerry cow, and he as big as a man!" screamed the girl.

"He was, the thief!" yelled the old woman. "I seen him firsht on the hill, cringeing behind a rock, and he hardly able to thrail the tail afther him!"

"Run now, like a good girl, and show me where did he cross the fence," said old Robert, puffing and blowing, as with a purple face he hurried into the yard to collect the hounds, who, like practised foragers, had already overrun the farmhouse, as was evidenced by an indignant and shrieking flight of fowls through the open door.

The girl ran, snatching off her red plaid shawl as she went.

"Here's the shpot now!" she called out, flinging the shawl down on the fence; "here's the very way just that he wint! Go south to the gap; I'll pull the pole out for ye--this is a cross place."

The hunt gratefully accepted her good offices. She tore the monstrous shaft of a cart out of a place that with it was impossible, and without it was a boggy scramble, and as we began to gallop again, I began to think there was a good deal to be said in favour of the New Woman.

I suppose we had had another quarter of an hour, when the mist, that had been hanging about all day, came down on us, and it was difficult to see more than a field ahead. We had got down on to lower ground, and we were in a sort of marshy hollow when we were confronted by the most serious obstacle of the day: a tall and obviously rotten bank clothed in briars, with sharp stones along its top, a wide ditch in front of it, and a disgustingly squashy take-off. Robert Trinder and the yellow horse held their course undaunted: the rest of the field turned as one man, and went for another way round--I, in my arrogance, followed the Master. The yellow horse rose out of the soft ground with quiet, indescribable ease, got a foothold on the side of the bank for his hind legs, and was away into the next field without pause or mistake.

"Go round, Captain!" shouted Trinder; "it's a bad place!"

I hardly heard him; I was already putting the filly at it for the second time. It took about three minutes for her to convince me that she and Robert were right, and I was wrong, and by that time everybody was out of sight, swallowed up in the mist. I tried round after the others, and found their footmarks up a lane and across a field; a loose stone wall confronted me, and I rode at it confidently; but the filly, soured by our recent encounter, reared and would have none of it. I tried yet another way round, and put her at a moderate and seemingly innocuous bank, at which, with the contrariety of her sex, she rushed at a thousand miles an hour. It looked somehow as if there might be a bit of a drop, but the filly had got her beastly blood up, and I have been in a better temper myself.

She rose to the jump when she was a good six feet from it. I knew she would not put an iron on it, and I sat down for the drop. It came with a vengeance. I had a glimpse of a thatched roof below me, and the next instant we were on it or in it--I don't know which. It gave way with a crash of rafters, the mare's forelegs went in, and I was shot over her head, rolled over the edge of the roof, and fell on my face into a manure heap. A yell and a pig burst simultaneously from the door, a calf followed, and while I struggled up out of my oozy resting-place, I was aware of the filly's wild face staring from the door of the shed in which she so unexpectedly found herself. The broken reins trailed round her legs, she was panting and shivering, and blood was trickling down the white blaze on her nose. I got her out through the low doorway with a little coaxing, and for a moment hardly dared to examine as to the amount of damage done. She was covered with cobwebs and dirt out of the roof, and, as I led her forward, she went lame on one foreleg; but beyond this, and a good many scratches, there was nothing wrong. My own appearance need not here be dilated upon. I was cleaning off what they call in Ireland "the biggest of the filth" with a bunch of heather, when from a cottage a little bit down the lane in which I was standing a small barelegged child emerged. It saw me, uttered one desperate howl, and fled back into the house. I abandoned my toilet and led the mare to the cottage door.

"Is any one in?" I said to the house at large.

A fresh outburst of yells was the sole response; there was a pattering of bare feet, and somewhere in the smoky gloom a door slammed. It was clearly a case of "Not at Home" in its conventional sense. I scribbled Robert Trinder's name on one of my visiting cards, laid it and half a sovereign on a table by the door, and started to make my way home.

The south of Ireland is singularly full of people. I do not believe you can go a quarter of a mile on any given road without meeting some one, and that some one is sure to be conversationally disposed and glad of the chance of answering questions. By dint of asking a good many, I eventually found myself on the high road, with five miles between me and Lisangle. The mare's lameness had nearly worn off, and she walked beside me like a dog. After all, I thought, I had had the best of the day, had come safely out of what might have been a nasty business, and was supplied with a story on which to dine out for the rest of my life. My only anxiety was as to whether I could hope for a bath when I got in--a luxury that had been hideously converted by the *locale* of my fall into a necessity. I led the filly in the twilight down the dark Lisangle drive, feeling all the complacency of a man who knows he has gone well in a strange country, and was just at the turn to the yard when I came upon an extraordinary group. All the women of the household were there, gathered in a tight circle round some absorbing central fact; all were shrieking at the tops of their voices, and the turkey cock in the yard gobbled in response to each shriek.

"Ma'am, ma'am!" I heard, "ye'll pull the tail off him!"

"Twisht the tink-an now, Bridgie! Twisht it!"

"Holy Biddy! the masther'll kill us!"

What the deuce were they at? and what was a "tink-an"? I dragged the filly nearer, and discovered that a hound puppy was the central point of the tumult, and was being contended for, like the body of Moses, by Miss Trinder and Bridgie the parlour-maid. Both were seated on the ground pulling at the puppy for all they were worth; Miss Trinder had him by the back of his neck and his tail, while Bridgie was dragging--what *was* she dragging at? Then I saw that the puppy's head was jammed in a narrow-necked tin milk-can, and that, as things were going, he would wear it, like the Man in the Iron Mask, for the rest of his life.

The small, grim face of Robert's aunt was scarlet with exertion; her black bonnet had slipped off her head, and the thin grey hair that was ordinarily wound round her little skull as tightly as cotton on a reel, was hanging in scanty wisps from its central knot; nevertheless, she was, metaphorically speaking, pulling Bridgie across the line every time. I gave the filly to one of the audience, and took Bridgie's place at the "tink-an". Miss Trinder and I put our backs into it, and suddenly I found myself flat on mine, with the "tink-an" grasped in both hands above my head.

A composite whoop of triumph rose from the spectators, and the filly rose with it. She went straight up on her hind legs, and the next instant she was away across the drive and into the adjoining field, and, considering all things, I don't blame her. We all ran after her. I led, and the various female retainers strung out after me like a flight of wild-duck, uttering cries of various encouragement and consternation. Miss Trinder followed, silent and indomitable, at the heel of the hunt, and the released puppy, who had also harked in, could be heard throwing his tongue in the dusky shrubbery ahead of us. It was all exasperatingly absurd, as things seem to have a habit of being in Ireland. I never felt more like a fool in my life, and the bitterest part of it was that it was all I could do to keep ahead of Bridgie. As for the filly, she waited till we got near her, and then she jumped a five-foot coped wall into the road, fell, picked herself up, and clattered away into darkness. At this point I heard Robert's horn, and sundry confused shouts and sounds informed me that the filly had run into the hounds.

She was found next day on the farm where she was bred, fifteen miles away. The farmer brought her back to Lisangle. She had injured three hounds, upset two old women and a donkey-cart, broken a gate, and finally, on arriving at the place of her birth, had, according to the farmer, "fired the divil's pelt of a kick into her own mother's stomach". Moreover, she "hadn't as much sound skin on her as would bait a rat-trap"--I here quote Mr. Trinder--and she had fever in all her feet.

Of course I bought her. I could hardly do less. I told Robert he might give her to the hounds, but he sent her over to me in a couple of months as good as new, and I won the regimental steeplechase cup with her last April.

A NINETEENTH-CENTURY MIRACLE

Captain "Pat" Naylor, of the --th Dragoons, had the influenza. For three days he had lain prostrate, a sodden and aching victim to the universal leveller, and an intolerable nuisance to his wife. This last is perhaps an over-statement; Mrs. Naylor was in the habit of bearing other people's burdens with excellent fortitude, but she felt justly annoyed that Captain Pat should knock up before they had fairly settled down in their new quarters, and while yet three of the horses were out of sorts after the crossing from England.

Pilot, however, was quite fit, a very tranquillising fact, and one that Mrs. Pat felt was due to her own good sense in summering him on her father's broad pastures in Meath, instead of "lugging him to Aldershot with the rest of the string, as Pat wanted to do," as she explained to Major Booth. Major Booth shed a friendly grin upon his fallen comrade, who lay, a deplorable object, on the horrid velvet-covered sofa peculiar to indifferent lodgings, and said vaguely that one of his brutes was right anyhow, and he was going to ride him at Carnfother the next day.

"You'd better come too, Mrs. Pat," he added; "and if you'll drive me I'll send my chap on with the horses. It's too far to ride. It's fourteen Irish miles off; and fourteen Irish miles is just about the longest distance I know."

Carnfother is a village in a remote part of the Co. Cork; it possesses a small hotel--in Ireland no hostelry, however abject, would demean itself by accepting the title of inn--a police barrack, a few minor public-houses, a good many dirty cottages, and an unrivalled collection of loafers. The stretch of salmon river that gleamed away to the distant heathery hills afforded the *raison d'etre* of both hotel and loafers, but the fishing season had not begun, and the attention of both was therefore undividedly bestowed on Mrs. Naylor and Major Booth. The former's cigarette and the somewhat Paradisaic dimensions of her apron skirt would indeed at any time have rivalled in interest the landing of a 20-lb. fish, and as she strode into the hotel the bystanders' ejaculatory piety would have done credit to a revival meeting.

"Well, well, I'll say nothing for her but that she's quare!" said the old landlady, hurrying in from her hens to attend to these rarer birds whom fortune had sent to her net.

Mrs. Pat's roan cob had attacked and defeated the fourteen Irish miles with superfluous zeal, and there were still several minutes before the hounds could be reasonably expected on the scene. The soda was bad, the whisky was worse. The sound of a riddle came in with the sunshine through the open door, and our friends strolled out into the street to see what was going on. In the centre of a ring of on-lookers an old man was playing, and was, moreover, dancing to his own music, and dancing with serious, incongruous elegance. Round and round the circle he footed it, his long thin legs twinkling in absolute accord with the complicated jig that his long thin fingers were ripping out of the cracked and raucous fiddle. A very plain, stout young woman, with a heavy red face and discordantly golden hair, shuffled round after him in a clumsy pretence of dancing, and as the couple faced Mrs. Pat she saw that the old man was blind. Steam was rising from his domed bald head, and his long black hair danced on his shoulders. His face was pale and strange and entirely self-absorbed. Had Mrs. Pat been in the habit of instituting romantic parallels between the past and the present she might have thought of the priests of Baal who danced in probably just such measures round the cromlechs in the hills above Carnfother; as she wasn't, she remarked merely that this was all very well, but that the old maniac would have to clear out of that before they brought Pilot round, or there'd be trouble.

There was trouble, but it did not arise from Pilot, but from the yellow-haired woman's pertinacious demands for money from Mrs. Naylor. She had the offensive fluency that comes of long practice in alternate wheedling and bullying, and although Major Booth had given her a shilling she continued to pester Mrs. Pat for a further largesse. But, as it happened, Mrs. Pat's purse was in her covert coat in the dog-cart, and Mrs. Pat's temper was ever within easy reach, and on being too closely pressed for the one she exhibited the other with a decision that contracted the ring of bystanders to hear the fun, and loosened the yellow-haired woman's language, till unfortunate Major Booth felt that if he could get her off the field of battle for a sovereign it would be cheap at the price. The old man continued to walk round and round, fingering a dumb tune on his fiddle that he did not bow, while the sunlight glistened hot and bright in his unwinking eyes; there was a faint smile on his lips, he heard as little as he saw; it was evident that he was away where "beyond these voices there is peace," in the fairy country that his forefathers called the Tir na'n Oge.

At this juncture the note of the horn sounded very sweetly from across the shining ford of the river. Hounds and riders came splashing up into the village street, the old man and his daughter were hustled to one side, and Mrs. Pat's affability returned as she settled her extremely smart little person on Pilot's curveting back, and was instantly aware that there was nothing present that could touch either of them in looks or quality. Carnfother was at the extreme verge of the D----Hounds' country; there were not more than about thirty riders out, and Mrs. Pat was not far wrong when she observed to Major Booth that there was not much class about them. Of the four or five women who were of the field, but one wore a habit with any pretensions to conformity with the sacred laws of fashion, and its colour was a blue that, taken in connection with a red, brass-buttoned waistcoat, reminded the severe critic from Royal Meath of the head porter at the Shelburne Hotel. So she informed Major Booth in one of the rare intervals permitted to her by Pilot for conversation.

"All right," responded that gentleman, "you wait until you and that ramping brute of yours get up among the stone walls, and you'll be jolly glad if she'll call a cab for you and see you taken safe home. I tell you what--you won't be able to see the way she goes."

"Rubbish!" said Mrs. Pat, and, whether from sympathy or from a petulant touch of her heel, Pilot at this moment involved himself in so intricate a series of plunges and bucks as to preclude further discussion.

The first covert--a small wood on the flank of a hill--was blank, and the hounds moved on across country to the next draw. It was a land of pasture, and in every fence was a deep muddy passage, through which the field splashed in single file with the grave stolidity of the cows by whom the gaps had been made. Mrs. Pat was feeling horribly bored. Her escort had joined himself to two of the ladies of the hunt, and though it was gratifying to observe that one wore a paste brooch in her tie and the other had an imitation cavalry bit and bridle, with a leather tassel hanging from her pony's throat, these things lost their savour when she had no one with whom to make merry over them. She had left her sandwiches in the dog-cart, her servant had mistaken whisky for sherry when he was filling her flask; the day had clouded over, and already one brief but furious shower had scourged the curl out of her dark fringe and made the reins slippery.

At last, however, a nice-looking gorse covert was reached, and the hounds threw themselves into it with promising alacrity. Pilot steadied himself, and stood with pricked ears, giving an occasional snatch at his bit, and looking, as no one knew better than his rider, the very picture of a hunter, while he listened for the first note that should tell of a find. He had not long to wait. There came a thin little squeal from the middle of the covert, and a hound flung up out of the thicker gorse and began to run along a ridge of rock, with head down, and feathering stern.

"They've got him, my lady," said a young farmer on a rough three-year-old to Mrs. Pat, as he stuffed his pipe in his pocket. "That's Patience; we'll have a hunt out o' this."

Then came another and longer squeal as Patience plunged out of sight again, and then, as the glowing chorus rose from the half-seen pack, a whip, posted on a hillside beyond the covert, raised his cap high in the air, and a wild screech that set Pilot dancing from leg to leg broke from a country boy who was driving a harrow in the next field: "Ga--aane awa--ay!"

Mrs. Pat forgot her annoyances. Her time had come. She would show that idiot Booth that Pilot was not to be insulted with impunity, and--But here retrospect and intention became alike merged in the present, and in the single resolve to get ahead and stay there. Half a dozen of Pilot's great reaching strides, and she was in the next field and over the low bank without putting an iron on it. The horse with the harrow, deserted by his driver, was following the hunt with the best of them, and, combining business with pleasure, was, as he went, harrowing the field with absurd energy. The Paste Brooch and the Shelburne Porter--so Mrs. Pat mentally distinguished them--were sailing along with a good start, and Major Booth was close at their heels. The light soil of the tilled field flew in every direction as thirty or more horses raced across it, and the usual retinue of foot runners raised an ecstatic yell as Mrs. Pat forged ahead and sent her big horse over the fence at the end of the field in a style that happily combined swagger with knowledge.

The hounds were streaking along over a succession of pasture fields, and the cattle gaps which were to be found in every fence vexed the proud soul of Mrs. Pat. She was too good a sportswoman to school her horse over needless jumps when hounds were running, but it infuriated her to have to hustle with these outsiders for her place at a gap. So she complained to Major Booth, with a vehemence of adjective that, though it may be forgiven to her, need not be set down here.

"Is *all* the wretched country like this?" she inquired indignantly, as the Shelburne Porter's pony splashed ahead of her through a muddy ford, just beyond which the hounds had momentarily checked; "you told me to bring out a big-jumped horse, and I might have gone the whole hunt on a bicycle!"

Major Booth's reply was to point to the hounds. They had cast back to the line that they had flashed over, and had begun to run again at right angles from the grassy valley down which they had come, up towards the heather-clad hills that lay back of Carnfother.

"Say your prayers, Mrs. Pat!" he said, in what Mrs. Pat felt to be a gratuitously offensive manner, "and I'll ask the lady in the pretty blue habit to have an eye to you. This is a hill fox and he's going to make you and Pilot sit up!"

Mrs. Pat was not in a mood to be trifled with, and I again think it better to omit her response to this inconvenient jesting. What she did was to give Pilot his head, and she presently found herself as near the hounds as was necessary, galloping in a line with the huntsman straight for a three-foot wall, lightly built of round stones. That her horse could refuse to jump it was a possibility that did not so much as enter her head; but that he did so was a fact whose stern logic could not be gainsaid. She had too firm a seat to be discomposed by the swinging plunge with which he turned from it, but her mental balance sustained a serious shake. That Pilot, at the head of the hunt should refuse, was a thing that struck at the root of her dearest beliefs. She stopped him and turned him at the wall again; again he refused, and at the same instant Major Booth and the blue habit jumped it side by side.

"What did I tell you!" the former called back, with a laugh that grated on Mrs. Pat's ear with a truly fiendish rasp; "do you want a lead?"

The incensed Mrs. Pat once more replied in forcible phraseology, as she drove her horse again at the wall. The average Meath horse likes stones just about as much as the average Co. Cork horse enjoys water, and the train of running men and boys were given the exquisite gratification of a contest between Pilot and his rider.

"Howld on, miss, till I knock a few shtones for ye!" volunteered one, trying to interpose between Pilot and the wall.

"Get out of the way!" was Mrs. Pat's response to this civility, as she crammed her steed at the jump again. The volunteer, amid roars of laughter from his friends, saved his life only by dint of undignified agility, as the big horse whirled round, rearing and plunging.

"Isn't he the divil painted?" exclaimed another in highest admiration; "wait till I give him a couple of slaps of my bawneen, miss!" He dragged off his white flannel coat and attacked Pilot in the rear with it, while another of the party flung clods of mud vaguely into the battle, and another persistently implored the maddened Mrs. Pat to get off and let him lead the horse over "before she'd lose her life:" a suggestion that has perhaps a more thoroughly exasperating effect than any other on occasions such as this.

By the time that Pilot had pawed down half the wall and been induced to buck over, or into, what remained of it, Mrs. Pat's temper was irretrievably gone, and she was at the heel instead of the head of the hunt. Thanks to this position there was bestowed on her the abhorred, but not to be declined, advantage of availing herself of the gaps made in the next couple of jumps by the other riders; but the stones they had kicked down were almost as agitating to Pilot's ruffled nerves as those that still remained in position. She found it the last straw that she should have to wait for the obsequious runners to tear these out of her way, while the galloping backs in front of her grew smaller and smaller, and the adulatory condolences of her assistants became more and more hard to endure. She literally hurled the shilling at them as she set off once more to try to recover her lost ground, and by sheer force of passion hustled Pilot over the next broken-down wall without a refusal. For she had now got into that stony country whereof Major Booth had spoken. Rough heathery fields, ribbed with rocks and sown with grey boulders, were all round. The broad salmon river swept sleekly through the valley below, among the bland green fields which were as far away for all practical purposes as the plains of Paradise. No one who has not ridden a stern chase over rough ground on a well-bred horse with his temper a bit out of hand will be able at all fitly to sympathise with the trials of Mrs.

Naylor. The hunt and all that appertained to it had sunk out of sight over a rugged hillside, and she had nothing by which to steer her course save the hoof-marks in the occasional black and boggy intervals between the heathery knolls. No one had ever accused her of being short of pluck, and she pressed on her difficult way with the utmost gallantry; but short of temper she certainly was, and at each succeeding obstacle there ensued a more bitter battle between her and her horse. Every here and there a band of crisp upland meadow would give the latter a chance, but each such advantage would be squandered in the war dance that he indulged in at every wall.

At last the summit of the interminable series of hills was gained, and Mrs. Pat scanned the solitudes that surrounded her with wrathful eyes. The hounds were lost, as completely swallowed up as ever were Korah, Dathan and Abiram. Not the most despised of the habits or the feeblest of the three-year-olds had been left behind to give a hint of their course; but the hoof-marks showed black on a marshy down-grade of grass, and with an angry clout of her crop on Pilot's unaccustomed ribs, she set off again. A narrow road cut across the hills at the end of the field. The latter was divided from it by a low, thin wall of sharp slaty stones, and on the further side there was a wide and boggy drain. It was not a nice place, and Pilot thundered down towards it at a pace that suited his rider's temper better than her judgment. It was evident, at all events, that he did not mean to refuse. Nor did he; he rose out of the heavy ground at the wall like a rocketing pheasant, and cleared it by more than twice its height; but though he jumped high he did not jump wide, and he landed half in and out of the drain, with his forefeet clawing at its greasy edge, and his hind legs deep in the black mud.

Mrs. Pat scrambled out of the saddle with the speed of light, and after a few momentous seconds, during which it seemed horribly likely that the horse would relapse bodily into the drain, his and Mrs. Pat's efforts prevailed, and he was standing, trembling, and dripping, on the narrow road. She led him on for a few steps; he went sound, and for one delusive instant she thought he had escaped damage; then, through the black slime on one of his hind legs the red blood began to flow. It came from high up inside the off hind leg, above the hock, and it welled ever faster and faster, a plaited crimson stream that made his owner's heart sink. She dipped her handkerchief in the ditch and cleaned the cut. It was deep in the fleshy part of the leg, a gaping wound, inflicted by one of those razor slates that hide like sentient enemies in such boggy places. It was large enough for her to put her hand in; she held the edges together, and the bleeding ceased for an instant; then, as she released them, it began again worse than ever. Her handkerchief was as inadequate for any practical purpose as ladies' handkerchiefs generally are, but an inspiration came to her. She tore off her gloves, and in a few seconds the long linen hunting-scarf that had been pinned and tied with such skilled labour in the morning was being used as a bandage for the wound. But though Mrs. Pat could tie a tie with any man in the regiment, she failed badly as a bandager of a less ornamental character. The hateful stream continued to pump forth from the cut, incarnadining the muddy road, and in despair she took Pilot by the head and began to lead him down the hill towards the valley.

Another gusty shower flung itself at her. It struck her bare white neck with whips of ice, and though she turned up the collar of her coat, the rain ran down under the neckband of her shirt and chilled her through and through. It was evident that an artery had been cut in Pilot's leg; the flow, from the wound never ceased; the hunting-scarf drenched with blood, had slipped down to the hock. It seemed to Mrs. Pat that her horse must bleed to death, and, tough and unemotional though she was, Pilot was very near her heart; tears gathered in her eyes as she led him slowly on through the rain and the loneliness, in the forlorn hope of finding help. She progressed in this lamentable manner for perhaps half a mile; the rain ceased, and she stopped to try once more to readjust the scarf, when, in the stillness that had followed the cessation of the rain, she heard a faint and distant sound of music. It drew nearer, a thin, shrill twittering, and as Mrs. Pat turned quickly from her task to see what this could portend, she heard a woman's voice say harshly:--

"Ah, have done with that thrash of music; sure, it'll be dark night itself before we're in to Lismore."

There was something familiar in the coarse tones. The weirdness fell from the wail of the music as Mrs. Pat remembered the woman who had bothered her for money that morning in Carnfother. She and the blind old man were tramping slowly up the road, seemingly as useless a couple to any one in Mrs. Pat's plight as could well be imagined.

"How far am I from Carnfother?" she asked, as they drew near to her. "Is there any house near here?"

"There is not," said the yellow-haired woman; "and ye're four miles from Carnfother yet."

"I'll pay you well if you will take a message there for me--" began Mrs. Pat.

"Are ye sure have ye yer purse in yer pocket?" interrupted the yellow-haired woman with a laugh that succeeded in being as nasty as she wished; "or will I go dancin' down to Carnfother--"

"Have done, Joanna!" said the old man suddenly; "what trouble is on the lady? What lamed the horse?"

He turned his bright blind eyes full on Mrs. Pat. They were of the curious green blue that is sometimes seen in the eyes of a grey collie, and with all Mrs. Pat's dislike and suspicion of the couple, she knew that he was blind.

"He was cut in a ditch," she said shortly.

The old man had placed his fiddle in his daughter's hands; his own hands were twitching and trembling.

"I feel the blood flowing," he said in a very low voice, and he walked up to Pilot.

His hands went unguided to the wound, from which the steady flow of blood had never ceased. With one he closed the lips of the cut, while with the other he crossed himself three times. His daughter watched him stolidly; Mrs. Pat, with a certain alarm, having, after the manner of her kind, explained to herself the incomprehensible with the all-embracing formula of madness. Yes, she thought, he was undoubtedly mad, and as soon as the paroxysm was past she would have another try at bribing the woman.

The old man was muttering to himself, still holding the wound in one hand. Mrs. Pat could distinguish no words, but it seemed to her that he repeated three times what he was saying. Then he straightened himself and stroked Pilot's quarter with a light, pitying hand. Mrs. Pat stared. The bleeding had ceased. The hunting-scarf lay on the road at the horse's empurpled hoof. There was nothing to explain the mystery, but the fact remained.

"He'll do now," said the blind man. "Take him on to Carnfother; but ye'll want to get five stitches in that to make a good job of it."

"But--I don't understand--" stammered Mrs. Pat, shaken for once out of her self-possession by this sudden extension of her spiritual horizon. "What have you done? Won't it begin again?" She turned to the woman in her bewilderment: "Is--is he mad?"

"For as mad as he is, it's him you may thank for yer horse," answered the yellow-haired woman. "Why, Holy Mother! did ye never hear of Kane the Blood-Healer?"

The road round them was suddenly thronged with hounds, snuffing at Pilot, and pushing between Mrs. Pat and the fence. The cheerful familiar sound of the huntsman's voice rating them made her feel her feet on solid ground again. In a moment Major Booth was there, the Master had dismounted, the habits, loud with sympathy and excitement, had gathered round; a Whip was examining the cut, while he spoke to the yellow-haired woman.

Mrs. Pat tie-less, her face splashed with mud, her bare hands stained with blood, told her story. It is, I think, a point in her favour that for a moment she forgot what her appearance must be.

"The horse would have bled to death before the lady got to Carnfother, sir," said the Whip to the Master; "it isn't the first time I seen life saved by that one. Sure, didn't I see him heal a man that got his leg in a mowing machine, and he half-dead, with the blood spouting out of him like two rainbows!"

This is not a fairy story. Neither need it be set lightly down as a curious coincidence. I know the charm that the old man said. I cannot give it here. It will only work successfully if taught by man to woman or by woman to man; nor do I pretend to say that it will work for every one. I believe it to be a personal and wholly incomprehensible gift, but that such a gift has been bestowed, and in more parts of Ireland than one, is a bewildering and indisputable fact.

HIGH TEA AT McKEOWN'S

P apa!" said the youngest Miss Purcell, aged eleven, entering the drawing-room at Mount Purcell in a high state of indignation and a flannel dressing-gown that had descended to her in unbroken line of succession from her eldest sister, "isn't it my turn for the foxy mare to-morrow? Nora had her at Kilmacabee, and it's a rotten shame--"

The youngest Miss Purcell here showed signs of the imminence of tears, and rooted in the torn pocket of the dressing-gown for the hereditary pocket-handkerchief that went with it.

Sir Thomas paused in the act of cutting the end off a long cigar, and said briefly:--

"Neither of you'll get her. She's going ploughing the Craughmore."

The youngest Miss Purcell knew as well as her sister Nora that the latter had already commandeered the foxy mare, and, with the connivance of the cowboy, had concealed her in the cow-house; but her sense of tribal honour, stimulated by her sister's threatening eye, withheld her from opening this branch of the subject.

"Well, but Johnny Mulcahy won't plough to-morrow because he's going to the Donovan child's funeral. Tommy Brien's just told me so, and he'll be drunk when he comes back, and to-morrow'll be the first day that Carnage and Trumpeter are going out--"

The youngest Miss Purcell paused, and uttered a loud sob.

"My darling baby," remonstrated Lady Purcell from behind a reading-lamp, "you really ought not to run about the stable-yard at this hour of the night, or, indeed, at any other time!"

"Baby's always bothering to come out hunting," remarked an elder sister, "and you know yourself, mamma, that the last time she came was when she stole the postman's pony, and he had to run all the way to Drinagh, and you said yourself she was to be kept in the next day for a punishment."

"How ready you are with your punishments! What is it to you if she goes out or no?" demanded Sir Thomas, whose temper was always within easy reach.

"She can have the cob, Tom," interposed stout and sympathetic Lady Purcell, on whom the tears of her youngest born were having their wonted effect, "I'll take the donkey chaise if I go out."

"The cob is it?" responded Sir Thomas, in the stalwart brogue in which he usually expressed himself. "The cob has a leg on him as big as your own since the last day one of them had him out!" The master of the house looked round with exceeding disfavour on his eight good-looking daughters. "However, I suppose it's as good to be hanged for a sheep as a lamb, and if you don't want him--"

The youngest Miss Purcell swiftly returned her handkerchief to her pocket, and left the room before any change of opinion was possible.

Mount Purcell was one of those households that deserve to be subsidised by any country neighbourhood in consideration of their unfailing supply of topics of conversation. Sir Thomas was a man of old family, of good income and of sufficient education, who, while reserving the power of comporting himself like a gentleman, preferred as a rule to assimilate his demeanour to that of one of his own tenants (with whom, it may be mentioned, he was extremely popular). Many young men habitually dined out on Sir Thomas's brogue and his unwearying efforts to dispose of his eight daughters.

His wife was a handsome, amiable, and by no means unintelligent lady upon whose back the eight daughters had ploughed and had left long furrows. She was not infrequently spoken of as "that un*for*tunate Lady Purcell!" with a greater or less broadening of the accent on the second syllable according to the social standard of the speaker. Her tastes were comprehended and sympathised with by her gardener, and by the clerk at Mudie's who refilled her box. The view taken of her by her husband and family was mainly a negative one, and was tinged throughout by the facts that she was afraid to drive anything more ambitious than the donkey, and had been known to mistake the kennel terrier for a hound puppy. She had succeeded in transmitting to her daughters her very successful complexion and blue eyes, but her responsibility for them had apparently gone no further. The Misses

Purcell faced the world and its somewhat excessive interest in them with the in-trepid ***esprit de corps*** of a square of British infantry, but among themselves they fought, as the coachman was wont to say--and no one knew better than the coach-man--"both bitther an regular, like man and wife!" They ranged in age from about five and twenty downwards, sportswomen, warriors, and buccaneers, all of them, and it would be difficult to determine whether resentment or a certain secret pride bulked the larger in their male parent's mind in connection with them.

"Are you going to draw Clashnacrona to-morrow?" asked Muriel, the second of the gang (Lady Purcell, it should have been mentioned, had also been responsible for her daughters' names), rising from her chair and pouring what was left of her after dinner coffee into her saucer, a proceeding which caused four pairs of lam-bent eyes to discover themselves in the coiled mat of red setters that occupied the drawing-room hearthrug.

"No, I am not," said Sir Thomas, "and, what's more, I'm coming in early. I'm a fool to go hunting at all at this time o' year, with half the potatoes not out of the ground." He rose, and using the toe of his boot as the coulter of a plough, made a way for himself among the dogs to the centre of the hearthrug. "Be hanged to these dogs! I declare I don't know am I more plagued with dogs or daughters! Lucy!"

Lady Purcell dutifully disinterred her attention from a catalogue of Dutch bulbs.

"When I get in to-morrow I'll go call on that Local Government Board Inspec-tor who's staying in Drinagh. They tell me he's a very nice fellow and he's rolling in money. I daresay I'll ask him to dinner. He was in the army one time, I believe. They often give these jobs to soldiers. If any of you girls come across him," he con-tinued, bending his fierce eyebrows upon his family, "I'll trouble you to be civil to him and show him none of your infernal airs because he happens to be an English-man! I hear he's bicycling all over the country and he might come out to see the hounds."

Rosamund, the eldest, delivered herself of an almost imperceptible wink in the direction of Violet, the third of the party. Sir Thomas's diplomacies were thor-oughly appreciated by his offspring. "It's time some of you were cleared out from under my feet!" he told them. Nevertheless when, some four or five years before, a subaltern of Engineers engaged on the Government survey of Ireland had laid his career, plus fifty pounds per annum and some impalpable expectations, at the feet of Muriel, the clearance effected by Sir Thomas had been that of Lieutenant Aubrey Hamilton. "Is it marry one of my daughters to that penniless pup!" he had said to Lady Purcell, whose sympathies had, as usual, been on the side of the detrimental. "Upon my honour, Lucy, you're a bigger fool than I thought you--and that's saying a good deal!"

It was near the beginning of September, and but a sleepy half dozen or so of riders had turned out to meet the hounds the following morning, at Liss Cranny Wood. There had been rain during the night and, though it had ceased, a wild wet wind was blowing hard from the north-west. The yellowing beech trees twisted and swung their grey arms in the gale. Hats flew down the wind like driven grouse; Sir Thomas's voice, in the middle of the covert, came to the riders assembled at the cross roads on the outskirts of the wood in gusts, fitful indeed, but not so fitful that Nora, on the distrained foxy mare, was not able to gauge to a nicety the state of his temper. From the fact of her unostentatious position in the rear it might safely be concluded that it, like the wind, was still rising. The riders huddled together in the lee of the trees, their various elements fused in the crucible of Sir Thomas's wrath into a compact and anxious mass. There had been an unusually large entry of puppies that season, and Sir Thomas's temper, never at its best on a morning of cubbing, was making exhaustive demands on his stock of expletives. Rabbits were flying about in every direction, each with a shrieking puppy or two in its wake. Jerry, the Whip, was galloping *ventre a terre* along the road in the vain endeavour to overtake a couple in headlong flight to the farm where they had spent their happier earlier days. At the other side of the wood the Master was blowing himself into apoplexy in the attempt to recall half a dozen who were away in full cry after a cur-dog, and a zealous member of the hunt looked as if he were playing polo with another puppy that doubled and dodged to evade the lash and the duty of getting to covert. Hither and thither among the beech trees went that selection from the Master's family circle, exclusive of the furtive Nora, that had on this occasion taken the field. It was a tradition in the country that there were never fewer than four Miss Purcells out, and that no individual Miss Purcell had more than three days' hunting in the season. Whatever may have been the truth of this, the companion legend that each Miss Purcell slept with two hound puppies in her bed was plausibly upheld by the devotion with which the latter clung to the heels of their nurses.

In the midst of these scenes of disorder an old fox rightly judging that this was no place for him, slid out of the covert, and crossed the road just in front of where Nora, in a blue serge skirt and a red Tam-o'-Shanter cap, lurked on the foxy mare. Close after him came four or five couple of old hounds, and, prominent among her elders, yelped the puppy that had been Nora's special charge. This was not cubbing, and no one knew it better than Nora; but the sight of Carnage among the prophets--Carnage, whose noblest quarry hitherto had been the Mount Purcell turkey-cock--overthrew her scruples. The foxy mare, a ponderous creature, with a mane like a Nubian lion and a mouth like steel, required nearly as much room to turn in as a man-of-war, and while Nora, by vigorous use of her heel and a reliable ash plant, was getting her head round, her sister Muriel, on a raw-boned well-bred colt--Sir Thomas, as he said, made the best of a bad job, and utilised his daughters as roughriders--shot past her down the leafy road, closely followed by a stranger on a weedy bay horse, which Nora instantly recognised as the solitary hireling of the; neighbourhood.

Through the belt of wood and out into the open country went the five couple, and after them went Muriel, Nora and the strange man. There had been an instant when the colt had thought that it seemed a pity to leave the road, but, none the less, he had the next instant found himself in the air, a considerable distance above a low stone wall, with a tingling streak across his ribs, and a bewildering sensation of having been hustled. The field in which he alighted was a sloping one and he ramped down it very enjoyably to himself, with all the weight of his sixteen hands and a half concentrated in his head, when suddenly a tall grassy bank confronted him, with, as he perceived with horror, a ditch in front of it. He tried to swerve, but there seemed something irrevocable about the way in which the bank faced him, and if his method of "changing feet" was not strictly conventional, he achieved the main point and found all four safely under him when he landed, which was as much--if not more than as much--as either he or Muriel expected. The Miss Purcells were a practical people, and were thankful for minor mercies.

It was at about this point that the stranger on the hireling drew level; he had not been at the meet, and Muriel turned her head to see who it was that was kicking old McConnell's screw along so well. He lifted his cap, but he was certainly a stranger. She saw a discreetly clipped and pointed brown beard, with a rather long and curling moustache.

"Fed on furze!" thought Muriel, with a remembrance of the foxy mare's upper lip when she came in "off the hill".

Then she met the strange man's eyes--was he quite a stranger? What was it about the greeny-grey gleam of them that made her heart give a curious lift, and then sent the colour running from it to her face and back again to her heart?

"I thought you were going to cut me--Muriel!" said the strange man.

In the meantime the five couple and Carnage were screaming down the heathery side of Liss Cranny Hill, on a scent that was a real comfort to them after nearly five miserable months of kennels and road-work, and a glorious wind under their sterns. Jerry, the Whip, was riding like a madman to stop them; they knew that well, and went the faster for it. Sir Thomas was blowing his horn inside out. But Jerry was four fields behind, and Sir Thomas was on the wrong side of the wood, and Miss Muriel and the strange gentleman were coming on for all they were worth, and were as obviously bent on having a good time as they were. Carnage flung up her handsome head and squealed with pure joy, as she pitched herself over the big bounds fence at the foot of the hill, and flopped across the squashy ditch on the far side. There was grass under her now, beautiful firm dairy grass, and that entrancing perfume was lying on it as thick as butter--Oh! it was well to be hunting! thought Carnage, with another most childish shriek, legging it after her father and mother and several other blood relations in a way that did Muriel's heart good to see.

The fox, as good luck would have it, had chosen the very pick of Sir Thomas's country, and Muriel and the stranger had it all to themselves. She looked over her shoulder. Away back in a half-dug potato field Nora and a knot of labourers were engaged in bitter conflict with the foxy mare on the subject of a bank with a rivulet in front of it. To refuse to jump running water had been from girlhood the resolve of the foxy mare; it was plain that neither Nora's ash plant, nor the stalks of rag-wort, torn from the potato ridges, with which the countrymen flagellated her from behind, were likely to make her change her mind. Farther back still were a few specks, motionless apparently, but representing, as Muriel was well aware, the speeding indignant forms of those Miss Purcells who had got left. As for Sir Thomas--well, it was no good going to meet the devil half-way! was the filial reflection; of

Sir Thomas's second daughter, as, with a clatter of stones, she and the colt dropped into a road, and charged on over the bank on the other side, the colt leaving a hind leg behind him in it, and sending thereby a clod of earth flying into the stranger's face. The stranger only laughed, and catching hold of the much enduring hireling he drove him level with the colt, and lifted him over the ensuing bank and gripe in a way subsequently described by Jerry as having "covered acres".

But the old fox's hitherto straight neck was getting a twist in it. Possibly he had summered himself rather too well, and found himself a little short of training for the point that he had first fixed on. At all events, he swung steadily round, and headed for the lower end of the long belt of Liss Cranny Wood; and, as he and his pursuers so headed, Retributive Justice, mounted on a large brown horse, very red in the face, and followed by a string of hounds and daughters, galloped steadily toward the returning sinners.

It is probably superfluous to reproduce for sporting readers the exact terms in which an infuriated master of hounds reproves an erring flock. Sir Thomas, even under ordinary circumstances, had a stirring gift of invective. It was currently reported that after each day's hunting Lady Purcell made a house-to-house visitation of conciliation to all subscribers of five pounds and upwards. On this occasion the Master, having ordered his two daughters home without an instant's delay, proceeded to a satiric appreciation of the situation at large and in detail, with general reflections as to the advantage to tailors of sticking to their own trade, and direct references of so pointed a character to the mental abilities of the third delinquent, that that gentleman's self-control became unequal to further strain, and he also retired abruptly from the scene.

Nora and Muriel meanwhile pursued their humbled, but unrepentant, way home. It was blowing as hard as ever. Muriel's hair had only been saved from complete overthrow by two hair-pins yielded, with pelican-like devotion, by a sister. Nora had lost the Tam-o'-Shanter, and had torn her blue serge skirt. The foxy mare had cast a shoe, and the colt was unaffectedly done.

"He's mad for a drink!" said Muriel, as he strained towards the side of the bog road, against which the waters of a small lake, swollen by the recent rains, were washing in little waves under the lash of the wind--"I think I'll let him just wet his mouth."

She slackened the reins, and the thirsty colt eagerly thrust his muzzle into the water. As he did so he took another forward step, and instantly, with a terrific splash, he and his rider were floundering in brown water up to his withers in the ditch below the submerged edge of the road. To Muriel's credit it, must be said that she bore this unlooked-for immersion with the nerve of a Baptist convert. In a second she had pulled the colt round parallel with the bank, and in another she had hurled herself from the saddle and was dragging herself, like a wounded otter, up on to the level of the road.

"Well you've done it now, Muriel!" said Nora dispassionately. "How pleased Sir Thomas will be when the colt begins to cough to-morrow morning! He's bound to catch cold out of this. Look out! Here's that man that went the run with us. I'd try and wipe some of the mud off my face if I were you!"

A younger sister of fifteen is not apt to err on the side of over sympathy, but the deficiencies of Nora were more than made up for by the solicitude of the stranger with the pointed beard. He hauled the colt from his watery nest, he dried him down with handfuls of rushes, he wiped the saddle with his own beautiful silk pocket-handkerchief. For a stranger he displayed--so it struck Nora--a surprising knowledge of the locality. He pointed out that Mount Purcell was seven miles away, and that the village of Drinagh, where he was putting up--("Oho! so he's the inspector Sir Thomas was going to be so civil to!" thought the younger Miss Purcell with an inward grin)--was only two or three miles away.

"You know, Nora," said Muriel with an unusually conciliatory manner, "it isn't at all out of our way, and the colt *ought* to get a proper rub down and a hot drink."

"I should have thought he'd had about as much to drink as he wanted, hot or cold!" said Nora.

But Nora had not been a younger sister for fifteen years for nothing, and it was for Drinagh that the party steered their course.

Their arrival stirred McKeown's Hotel (so-called) to its depths. Destiny had decreed that Mrs. McKeown, being, as she expressed it, "an epicure about boots," should choose this day of all others to go to "town" to buy herself a pair, leaving the direction of the hotel in the hands of her husband, a person of minor importance, and of Mary Ann Whooly, a grey-haired kitchen-maid, who milked the cows and made the beds, and at a distance in the back-yard was scarcely distinguishable from the surrounding heaps of manure.

The Inspector's hospitality knew no limits, and failed to recognise that those of McKeown's Hotel were somewhat circumscribed. He ordered hot whisky and water, mutton chops, dry clothes for Miss Purcell, fires, tea, buttered toast, poached eggs and other delicacies simultaneously and immediately, and the voice of Mary Ann Whooly imploring Heaven's help for herself and its vengeance upon her inadequate assistants was heard far in the streets of Drinagh.

"Sure herself" (herself was Mrs. McKeown) "has her box locked agin me, and I've no clothes but what's on me!" she protested, producing after a long interval a large brown shawl and a sallow-complexioned blanket, "but the Captain's after sending these. Faith, they'll do ye grand! Arrah, why not, asthore! Sure he'll never look at ye!"

These consisted of a long covert coat, a still longer pair of yellow knitted stockings, and a pair of pumps.

"Sure they're the only best we have," continued Mary Ann Whooly, pooling, as it were, her wardrobe with that of the lodger. "God's will must be, Miss Muriel, my darlin' gerr'l!"

It says a good deal for the skill of Nora as a tire-woman that her sister's appearance ten minutes afterwards was open to no reproach, save possibly that of eccentricity, and the Inspector's gaze--which struck the tire-woman as being of a singularly enamoured character for so brief an acquaintance--was so firmly fixed upon her sister's countenance that nothing else seemed to signify. It was by this time past two o'clock, and the repast, which arrived in successive relays, had, at all events, the merit of || combining the leading features of breakfast, lunch and afternoon tea in one remarkable procession, Julia Connolly, having inaugurated the entertainment with tumblers of dark brown steaming whisky and water, was impelled from strength to strength by her growing sense of the greatness of the occasion, and it would be hard to say whether the younger Miss Purcell was more gratified by the mound of feather-light pancakes which followed on the tea and buttered toast, or by the almost cringing politeness of her elder sister.

"How civil she is!" thought Nora scornfully; "for all she's so civil she'll have to lend me her saddle next week, or I'll tell them the whole story!" (Them meant the sisterhood.) "I bet he was holding her hand just before the pancakes came in!"

At about this time Lady Purcell, pursuing her peaceful way home in her donkey chaise, was startled by the sound of neighing and by the rattle of galloping hoofs behind her, and her consternation may be imagined when the foxy mare and the colt, saddled but riderless, suddenly ranged up one on either side of her chaise. Having stopped themselves with one or two prodigious bounds that sent the mud flying in every direction, they proceeded to lively demonstrations of friendship towards the donkey, which that respectable animal received very symptom of annoyance. Lady Purcell had never in her life succeeded in knowing one horse from another, and what horses these were she had not the faintest idea; but the side saddles were suggestive of her Amazon brood; she perceived that one of the horses had been under water, and by the time she had arrived at her own hall door, with the couple still in close attendance upon her, anxiety as to the fate of her daughters and exhaustion from much scourging of the donkey, upon whom the heavy coquetries of the foxy mare had had a most souring effect, rendered the poor lady but just capable of asking if Sir Thomas had returned.

"He is, my Lady, but he's just after going down to the farm, and he's going on to call on the English gentleman that's at Mrs. McKeown's."

"And the young ladies?" gasped Lady Purcell.

The answer suited with her fears. Lady Purcell was not wont to take the initiative, still less one of her husband's horses, without his approval; but the thought of the saturated side-saddle lent her decision, and as soon as a horse and trap could be got ready she set forth for Drinagh.

It need not for a moment be feared that such experienced campaigners as the Misses Muriel and Nora Purcell had forgotten that their father had settled to call upon their temporary host, what time the business of the morning should be ended, or that they had not arranged a sound scheme of retirement, but when the news was brought to them that during the absence of the stable-boy--"to borrow a half score of eggs and a lemon for pancakes," it was explained--their horses had broken forth from the cowshed and disappeared, it may be admitted that even their stout hearts quailed.

"Oh, it will be all right!" the Inspector assured them, with the easy optimism of the looker-on in domestic tragedy; "your father will see there was nothing else for you to do."

"That's all jolly fine," returned Nora, "but *I'm* going out to borrow Casey's car" (Casey was the butcher), "and I'll just tell old Mary Ann to keep a sharp look out for Sir Thomas, and give us warning in time."

It is superfluous to this simple tale to narrate the conversation that befel on the departure of Nora. It was chiefly of a retrospective character, with disquisitions on such abstractions as the consolations that sometimes follow on the loss of a wealthy great-aunt, the difficulties of shaving with a "tennis elbow," the unchanging quality of certain emotions. This later topic was still under discussion when Nora burst into the room.

"Here's Sir Thomas!" she panted. "Muriel, fly! There's no time to get downstairs, but Mary Ann Whooly said we could go into the room off this sitting-room till he's gone."

Flight is hardly the term to be applied to the second Miss Purcell's retreat, and it says a good deal for the Inspector's mental collapse that he saw nothing ludicrous in her retreating back, clad as it was in his own covert coat, with a blanket like the garment of an Indian brave trailing beneath it. Nora tore open a door near the fireplace, and revealed a tiny room containing a table, a broken chair, and a heap of feathers near an old feather bed on the floor.

"Get in, Muriel!" she cried.

They got in, and as the door closed on them Sir Thomas entered the room.

During the morning the identity of the stranger on whom he had poured the vials of his wrath, with the Local Government Board Inspector whom he was prepared to be delighted to honour, had been brought home to Sir Thomas, and nothing could have been more handsome and complete than the apology that he now tendered. He generously admitted the temptation endured in seeing hounds get away with a good fox on a day devoted to cubbing, and even went so far as to suggest that possibly Captain Clarke--

"Hamilton-Clarke," said the Inspector.

"Had ridden so hard in order to stop them."

"Er--quite so," said the Inspector.

Something caused the dressing-room door to rattle, and Captain Hamilton-Clarke grew rather red.

"My wife and I hope," continued Sir Thomas, urbanely, "that you will come over to dine with us to-morrow evening, or possibly to-night."

He stopped. A trap drove rapidly up to the door, and Lady Purcell's voice was heard agitatedly inquiring "if Miss Muriel and Miss Nora were there? Casey had just told her--"

The rest of the sentence was lost.

"Why, that *is* my wife!" said Sir Thomas. "What the deuce does she want here?"

A strange sound came from behind the door of the dressing-room: something between a stifled cry and a laugh. The Inspector's ears became as red as blood. Then from within there was heard a sort of rush, and something fell against the door. There followed a wholly uncontrolled yell and a crash, and the door was burst open.

It has, I think, been mentioned that in the corner of the dressing-room in which the Misses Purcell had taken refuge there was on the floor the remains of a feather bed. The feathers had come out through a ragged hole in one corner of it; Nora, in the shock of hearing of Lady Purcell's arrival, trod on the corner of the bed and squeezed more of the feathers out of it. A gush of fluff was the result, followed by a curious and unaccountable movement in the bed, and then from the hole there came forth a corpulent and very mangy old rat. Its face was grey and scaly, and horrid pink patches adorned its fat person. It gave one beady glance at Nora, and proceeded with hideous composure to lope heavily across the floor towards the hole in the wall by which it had at some bygone time entered the room. But the hole had been nailed up, and as the rat turned to seek another way of escape the chair upon which Muriel had incontinently sprung broke down, depositing her and her voluminous draperies on top of the rat.

I cannot feel that Miss Purcell is to be blamed that at this moment all power of self-control, of reason almost, forsook her. Regardless of every other consideration, she snatched the blankets and the covert-coat skirts into one massive handful, and with, as has been indicated, a yell of housemaid stridency, flung herself against the door and dashed into the sitting-room, closely followed by Nora, and rather less closely by the rat. The latter alone retained its presence of mind, and without an instant's delay hurried across the room and retired by the half-open door. Immediately from the narrow staircase there arose a series of those acclaims that usually attend the progress of royalty, and, in even an intenser degree, of rats. There came a masculine shout, a shrill and ladylike scream, a howl from Mary Ann Whooly, accompanied by the clang and rattle of a falling coal box, and then Lady Purcell, pale and breathless, appeared at the doorway of the sitting-room.

"Sure the young ladies isn't in the house at all, your ladyship!" cried the pursuing voice of Mary Ann Whooly, faithful, even at this supreme crisis, to a lost cause.

Lady Purcell heard her not. She was aware only of her daughter Muriel, attired like a scarecrow in a cold climate, and of the attendant fact that the arm of the Local Government Board Inspector was encircling Muriel's waist, as far as circumstances and a brown woollen shawl would permit. Nora, leaning half-way out of the window, was calling at the top of her voice for Sir Thomas's terrier; Sir Thomas was very loudly saying nothing in particular, much as an angry elderly dog barks into the night. Lady Purcell wildly concluded that the party was rehearsing a charade--the last scene of a very vulgar charade.

"Muriel!" she exclaimed, "***what*** have you got on you? And who--" She paused and stared at the Inspector. "Good gracious!" she cried, "why, it's Aubrey Hamilton!"

THE BAGMAN'S PONY

When the regiment was at Delhi, a T.G. was sent to us from the 105th Lancers, a bagman, as they call that sort of globe-trotting fellow that knocks about from one place to another, and takes all the fun he can out of it at other people's expense. Scott in the 105th gave this bagman a letter of introduction to me, told me that he was bringing down a horse to run at the Delhi races; so, as a matter of course, I asked him to stop with me for the week. It was a regular understood thing in India then, this passing on the T.G. from one place to another; sometimes he was all right, and sometimes he was a good deal the reverse--in any case, you were bound to be hospitable, and afterwards you could, if you liked, tell the man that sent him that you didn't want any more from him.

The bagman arrived in due course, with a rum-looking roan horse, called the "Doctor"; a very good horse, too, but not quite so good as the bagman gave out that he was. He brought along his own grass-cutter with him, as one generally does in India, and the grass-cutter's pony, a sort of animal people get because he can carry two or three more of these beastly clods of grass they dig up for horses than a man can, and without much regard to other qualities. The bagman seemed a decentish sort of chap in his way, but, my word! he did put his foot in it the first night at mess; by George, he did! There was somehow an idea that he belonged to a wine merchant business in England, and the Colonel thought we'd better open our best cellar for the occasion, and so we did; even got out the old Madeira, and told the usual story about the number of times it had been round the Cape. The bagman took everything that came his way, and held his tongue about it, which was rather damping. At last, when it came to dessert and the Madeira, Carew, one of our fellows, couldn't stand it any longer--after all, it *is* aggravating if a man won't praise your best wine, no matter how little you care about his opinion, and the bagman was supposed to be a *connoisseur*.

"Not a bad glass of wine that," says Carew to him; "what do you think of it?"

"Not bad," says the bagman, sipping it, "Think I'll show you something better in this line if you'll come and dine with me in London when you're home next."

"Thanks," says Carew, getting as red as his own jacket, and beginning to splutter--he always did when he got angry--"this is good enough for me, and for most people here--"

"Oh, but nobody up here has got a palate left," says the bagman, laughing in a very superior sort of way.

"What do you mean, sir?" shouted Carew, jumping up. "I'll not have any d----d bagmen coming here to insult me!"

By George, if you'll believe me, Carew had a false palate, with a little bit of sponge in the middle, and we all knew it, *except the bagman*. There was a frightful shindy, Carew wanting to have his blood, and all the rest of us trying to prevent a row. We succeeded somehow in the end, I don't quite know how we managed it, as the bagman was very warlike too; but, anyhow, when I was going to bed that night I saw them both in the billiard room, very tight, leaning up against opposite ends of the billiard table, and making shoves at the balls--with the wrong ends of their cues, fortunately.

"He called me a d----d bagman," says one, nearly tumbling down with laughing.

"Told me I'd no palate," says the other, putting his head down on the table and giggling away there "best thing I ever heard in my life."

Every one was as good friends as possible next day at the races, and for the whole week as well. Unfortunately for the bagman his horse didn't pull off things in the way he expected, in fact he hadn't a look in--we just killed him from first to last. As things went on the bagman began to look queer and by the end of the week he stood to lose a pretty considerable lot of money, nearly all of it to me. The way we arranged these matters then was a general settling-up day after the races were over; every one squared up his books and planked ready money down on the nail, or if he hadn't got it he went and borrowed from some one else to do it with. The bagman paid up what he owed the others, and I began to feel a bit sorry for the fellow when he came to me that night to finish up. He hummed and hawed a bit, and then asked if I should mind taking an I.O.U. from him, as he was run out of the ready.

Of course I said, "All right, old man, certainly, just the same to me," though it's usual in such cases to put down the hard cash, but still--fellow staying in my house, you know--sent on by this pal of mine in the 11th--absolutely nothing else to be done.

Next morning I was up and out on parade as usual, and in the natural course of events began to look about for my bagman. By George, not a sign of him in his room, not a sign of him anywhere. I thought to myself, this is peculiar, and I went over to the stable to try whether there was anything to be heard of him.

The first thing I saw was that the "Doctor's" stall was empty.

"How's this?" I said to the groom; "where's Mr. Leggett's horse?"

"The sahib has taken him away this morning."

I began to have some notion then of what my I.O.U. was worth.

"The sahib has left his grass-cutter and his pony," said the *sais*, who probably had as good a notion of what was up as I had.

"All right, send for the grass-cutter," I said.

The fellow came up, in a blue funk evidently, and I couldn't make anything of him. Sahib this, and sahib that, and salaaming and general idiotcy--or shamming--I couldn't tell which. I didn't know a nigger then as well as I do now.

"This is a very fishy business," I thought to myself, "and I think it's well on the cards the grass-cutter will be out of this to-night on his pony. No, by Jove, I'll see what the pony's good for before he does that. Is the grass-cutter's pony there?" I said to the *sais*.

"He is there, sahib, but he is only a *kattiawa tattoo*," which is the name for a common kind of mountain pony.

I had him out, and he certainly was a wretched-looking little brute, dun with a black stripe down his back, like all that breed, and all bony and ragged and starved.

"Indeed, he is a *gareeb kuch kam ki nahin*," said the *sais*, meaning thereby a miserable beast, in the most intensified form, "and not fit to stand in the sahib's stable."

All the same, just for the fun of the thing, I put the grass-cutter up on him, and told him to trot him up and down. By George! the pony went like a flash of light-ning! I had him galloped next; same thing--fellow could hardly hold him. I opened my eyes, I can tell you, but no matter what way I looked at him I couldn't see where on earth he got his pace from. It was there anyhow, there wasn't a doubt about that. "That'll do," I said, "put him up. And you just stay here," I said to the grass-cutter; "till I hear from Mr. Leggett where you're to go to. Don't leave Delhi till you get orders from me."

It got about during the day that the bagman had disappeared, and had had a soft thing of it as far as I was concerned. The 112th were dining with us that night, and they all set to work to draw me after dinner about the business--thought themselves vastly witty over it.

"Hullo Paddy, so you're the girl he left behind him!" "Hear he went off with two suits of your clothes, one over the other." "Cheer up, old man; he's left you the grass-cutter and the pony, and what *he* leaves must be worth having, I'll bet!" and so on.

I suppose I'd had a good deal more than my share of the champagne, but all of a sudden I began to feel pretty warm.

"You're all d----d funny," I said, "but I daresay you'll find he's left me some-thing that *is* worth having."

"Oh, yes!" "Go on!" "Paddy's a great man when he's drunk," and a lot more of the same sort.

"I tell you what it is," said I, "I'll back the pony he's left here to trot his twelve miles an hour on the road."

"Bosh!" says Barclay of the 112th. "I've seen him, and I'll lay you a thousand rupees even he doesn't."

"Done!" said I, whacking my hand down on the table.

"And I'll lay another thousand," says another fellow.

"Done with you too," said I.

Every one began to stare a bit then.

"Go to bed, Paddy," says the Colonel, "you're making an exhibition of your-self."

"Thank you, sir; I know pretty well what I'm talking about," said I; but, by George, I began privately to think I'd better pull myself together a bit, and I got out my book and began to hedge--laid three to one on the pony to do eleven miles in the hour, and four to one on him to do ten--all the fellows delighted to get their money on. I was to choose my own ground, and to have a fortnight to train the pony, and by the time I went to bed I stood to lose about L1,000.

Somehow in the morning I didn't feel quite so cheery about things--one doesn't after a big night--one gets nasty qualms, both mental and the other kind. I went out to look after the pony, and the first thing I saw by way of an appetiser was Biddy, with a face as long as my arm. Biddy, I should explain, was a chap called Biddulph, in the Artillery; they called him Biddy for short, and partly, too, because he kept a racing stable with me in those days, I being called Paddy by every one, because I was Irish--English idea of wit--Paddy and Biddy, you see.

"Well," said he, "I hear you've about gone and done it this time. The 112th are going about with trumpets and shawms, and looking round for ways to spend that thousand when they get it. There are to be new polo ponies, a big luncheon, and a piece of plate bought for the mess, in memory of that benefactor of the regiment, the departed bagman. Well, now, let's see the pony. That's what I've come down for."

I'm hanged if the brute didn't look more vulgar and wretched than ever when he was brought out, and I began to feel that perhaps I was more parts of a fool than I thought I was. Biddy stood looking at him there with his under-lip stuck out.

"I think you've lost your money," he said. That was all, but the way he said it made me feel conscious of the shortcomings of every hair in the brute's ugly hide.

"Wait a bit," I said, "you haven't seen him going yet. I think he has the heels of any pony in the place."

I got a boy on to him without any more ado, thinking to myself I was going to astonish Biddy. "You just get out of his way, that's all," says I, standing back to let him start.

If you'll believe it, he wouldn't budge a foot!--not an inch--no amount of licking had any effect on him. He just humped his back, and tossed his head and grunted--he must have had a skin as thick as three donkeys! I got on to him myself and put the spurs in, and he went up on his hind legs and nearly came back with me--that was all the good I got of that.

"Where's the grass-cutter," I shouted, jumping off him in about as great a fury as I ever was in. "I suppose *he* knows how to make this devil go!"

"Grass-cutter went away last night, sahib. Me see him try to open stable door and go away. Me see him no more."

I used pretty well all the bad language I knew in one blast. Biddy began to walk away, laughin till I felt as if I could kick him.

"I'm going to have a front seat for this trotting match," he said, stopping to get his wind. "Spectators along the route requested to provide themselves with pitch-forks and fireworks, I suppose, in case the champion pony should show any of his engaging little temper. Never mind, old man, I'll see you through this, there's no use in getting into a wax about it. I'm going shares with you, the way we always do."

I can't say I responded graciously, I rather think I cursed him and everything else in heaps. When he was gone I began to think of what could be done.

"Get out the dog-cart," I said, as a last chance. "Perhaps he'll go in harness."

We wheeled the cart up to him, got him harnessed to it, and in two minutes that pony was walking, trotting, anything I wanted--can't explain why--one of the mysteries of horseflesh. I drove him out through the Cashmere Gate, passing Biddy on the way, and feeling a good deal the better for it, and as soon as I got on to the flat stretch of road outside the gate I tried what the pony could do. He went even better than I thought he could, very rough and uneven, of course, but still promising. I brought him home, and had him put into training at once, as carefully as if he was going for the Derby. I chose the course, took the six-mile stretch of road from the Cashmere gate to Sufter Jung's tomb, and drove him over it every day. It was a splendid course--level as a table, and dead straight for the most part--and after a few days he could do it in about forty minutes out and thirty-five back. People began to talk then, especially as the pony's look and shape were improving each day, and after a little time every one was planking his money on one way or another--Biddy putting on a thousand on his own account--still, I'm bound to say the odds were against the pony. The whole of Delhi got into a state of excitement about it, natives and all, and every day I got letters warning me to take care, as there might be foul play. The stable the pony was in was a big one, and I had a wall built across it, and put a man with a gun in the outer compartment. I bought all his corn myself, in feeds at a time, going here, there, and everywhere for it, never to the same place for two days together--I thought it was better to be sure than sorry, and there's no trusting a nigger.

The day of the match every soul in the place turned out, such crowds that I could scarcely get the dog-cart through when I drove to the Cashmere gate. I got down there, and was looking over the cart to see that everything was right, when a little half-caste *keranie*, a sort of low-class clerk, came up behind me and began talking to me in a mysterious kind of way, in that vile *chi-chi* accent one gets to hate so awfully.

"Look here, Sar," he said, "you take my car, Sar; it built for racing. I do much trot-racing myself"--mentioning his name--"and you go much faster my car, Sar."

I trusted nobody in those days, and thought a good deal of myself accordingly. I hadn't found out that it takes a much smarter man to know how to trust a few.

"Thank you," I said, "I think I'll keep my own, the pony's accustomed to it."

I think he understood quite well what I felt, but he didn't show any resentment.

"Well, Sar, you no trust my car, you let me see your wheels?"

"Certainly," I said "you may look at them," determined in my own mind I should keep my eye on him while he did.

He got out a machine for propping the axle, and lifted the wheel off the ground.

"Make the wheel go round," he said.

I didn't like it much, but I gave the wheel a turn. He looked at it till it stopped.

"You lose match if you take that car," he said, "you take my car, Sar."

"What do you mean?" said I, pretty sharply.

"Look here," he said, setting the wheel going again. "You see here, Sar, it die, all in a minute, it jerk, doesn't die smooth. You see *my* wheel, Sar."

He put the lift under his own, and started the wheel revolving. It took about three times as long to die as mine, going steady and silent and stopping imperceptibly, not so much as a tremor in it.

"Now, Sar!" he said, "you see I speak true, Sar. I back you two hundred rupee, if I lose I'm ruin, and I beg you, Sar, take my car! can no win with yours, mine match car."

"All right!" said I with a sort of impulse, "I'll take it." And so I did.

I had to start just under the arch of the Cashmere gate, by a pistol shot, fired from overhead. I didn't quite care for the look of the pony's ears while I was waiting for it--the crowd had frightened him a bit I think. By Jove, when the bang came he reared straight up, dropped down again and stuck his forelegs out, reared again when I gave him the whip, every second of course telling against me.

"Here, let me help you," shouted Biddy, jumping into the trap. His weight settled the business, down came the pony, and we went away like blazes.

The three umpires rode with us, one each side and one behind, at least that was the way at first, but I found the clattering of their hoofs made it next to impossible to hold the pony. I got them to keep back, and after that he went fairly steadily, but it was anxious work. The noise and excitement had told on him a lot, he had a tendency to break during all that six miles out, and he was in a lather before we got to Sufter Jung's tomb. There were a lot of people waiting for me out there, some ladies on horseback, too, and there was a coffee-shop going, with drinks of all kinds. As I got near they began to call out, "You're done, Paddy, thirty-four minutes gone already, you haven't the ghost of a chance. Come and have a drink and look pleasant over it."

I turned the pony, and Biddy and I jumped out. I went up to the table, snatched up a glass of brandy and filled my mouth with it, then went back to the pony, took him by the head, and sent a squirt of brandy up each nostril; I squirted the rest down his throat, went back to the table, swallowed half a tumbler of curacoa or something, and was into the trap and off again, the whole thing not taking more than twenty seconds.

The business began to be pretty exciting after that. You can see four miles straight ahead of you on that road; and that day the police had special orders to keep it clear, so that it was a perfectly blank, white stretch as far as I could see. You know how one never seems to get any nearer to things on a road like that, and there was the clock hanging opposite to me on the splash board; I couldn't look at it, but I could hear its beastly click-click through the trotting of the pony, and that was nearly as bad as seeing the minute hand going from pip to pip. But, by George, I pretty soon heard a worse kind of noise than that. It was a case of preserve me from my friends. The people who had gone out to Sufter Jung's tomb on horseback to meet me, thought it would be a capital plan to come along after me and see the fun, and encourage me a bit--so they told me afterwards. The way they encouraged me was by galloping till they picked me up, and then hammering along behind me like a troop of cavalry till it was all I could do to keep the pony from breaking.

"You've got to win, Paddy," calls out Mrs. Harry Le Bretton, galloping up alongside, "you promised you would!"

Mrs. Harry and I were great friends in those days--very sporting little woman, nearly as keen about the match as I was--but at that moment I couldn't pick my words.

"Keep back!" I shouted to her; "keep back, for pity's sake!"

It was too late--the next instant the pony was galloping. The penalty is that you have to pull up, and make the wheels turn in the opposite direction, and I just threw the pony on his haunches. He nearly came back into the cart, but the tremendous jerk gave the backward turn to the wheels and I was off again. Not even that kept the people back. Mrs. Le Bretton came alongside again to say something else to me, and I suddenly felt half mad from the clatter and the frightful strain of the pony on my arms.

"D----n it all! Le Bretton!" I yelled, as the pony broke for the second time, "can't you keep your wife away!"

They did let me alone after that--turned off the road and took a scoop across the plain, so as to come up with me at the finish--and I pulled myself together to do the last couple of miles. I could see that Cashmere gate and the Delhi walls ahead of me; 'pon my soul I felt as if they were defying me and despising me, just standing waiting there under the blazing sky, and they never seemed to get any nearer. It was like the first night of a fever, the whizzing of the wheels, the ding-dong of the pony's hoofs, the silence all round, the feeling of stress and insane hurrying on, the throbbing of my head, and the scorching heat. I'll swear no fever I've ever had was worse than that last two miles.

As I reached the Delhi walls I took one look at the clock. There was barely a minute left.

"By Jove!" I gasped, "I'm done!"

I shouted and yelled to the pony like a madman, to keep up what heart was left in the wretched little brute, holding on to him for bare life, with my arms and legs straight out in front of me. The gray wall and the blinding road rushed by me like a river--I scarcely knew what happened--I couldn't think of anything but the ticking of the clock that I was somehow trying to count, till there came the bang of a pistol over my head.

It was the Cashmere gate, and I had thirteen seconds in hand.

*   *   *   *   *

There was never anything more heard of the bagman. He can, if he likes, soothe his conscience with the reflection that he was worth a thousand pounds to me.

But Mrs. Le Bretton never quite forgave me.

AN IRISH PROBLEM

Conversation raged on the long flanks of the mail-car.

An elderly priest, with a warm complexion and a controversial under-lip, was expounding his native country to a fellow-traveller, with slight but irrepressible pulpit gestures of the hand. The fellow traveller, albeit lavender-hued from an autumn east wind, was obediently observing the anaemic patches of oats and barley, pale and thin, like the hair of a starving baby, and the huge slants of brown heather and turf bog, and was interjecting "Just so!" at decent intervals. Now and then, as the two tall brown mares slackened for a bout of collar-work at a hill, or squeezed slowly past a cart stacked high with sods of turf, we, sitting in silence, Irish wolves in the clothing of English tourists, could hear across the intervening pile of luggage and bicycles such a storm of conversation as bursts forth at a dinner-party after the champagne has twice gone round.

The brunt of the talk was borne by the old lady in the centre. Her broad back, chequered with red plaid, remained monumental in height and stillness, but there was that in the tremor of the steel spray in her bonnet that told of a high pressure of narrative. The bearded Dublin tourist on her left was but little behind her in the ardour of giving information. His wife, a beautifully dressed lady with cotton-wool in her ears, remained abstracted, whether from toothache, or exclusiveness, or mere wifely boredom, we cannot say. Among the swift shuttles of Irish speech the ponderous questions and pronouncements of an English fisherman drove their way. The talk was, we gathered, of sport and game laws and their administration.

"Is it hares?" cried the Dublin tourist, perorating after a flight or two into the subject of poachers; "what d'ye think would happen a hare in Donegal?"

His handsome brown eye swept his audience, even, through the spokes of a bicycle, gathering in our sympathies. It left no doubts as to the tragedy that awaited the hare.

The east wind hunted us along the shore of the wide, bleak bay, rimmed with yellow sea-weed, and black and ruffled like the innumerable lakelets that lay along our route. The tall mountain over it was hooded in cloud. It seemed as threatening and mysterious as Sinai; ready to utter some awful voice of law to the brown solitudes and windy silences.

Far ahead of us a few houses rose suddenly above the low coast line, an ugly family party of squat gables and whitewashed walls, with nothing nearer them to westward than the homesteads of America.

Far and near there was not a tree visible, nor a touch of colour to tell of the saving grace of flowers. The brown mares swung the car along with something resembling enthusiasm; Letterbeg was the end of their stage; it was the end of ours also. Numb with long sitting we dropped cumbrously to earth from the high footboard, and found ourselves face to face with the problem of how to spend the next three hours. It was eleven o'clock in the morning, too early for lunch, though, apparently, quite the fashionable hour in Letterbeg for bottled porter, judging by the squeak of the corkscrew and the clash of glasses that issued from the dark interior of the house in front of which we had been shed by the mail-car. This was a long cottage with a prosperous slate roof, and a board over its narrow door announcing that one Jas. Heraty was licensed for the retail of spirits and porter.

The mail-car rolled away; as it crawled over the top of a hill and sank out of sight a last wave of the priestly hand seemed to include us. Doubtless we were being expounded as English tourists, and our great economic value to the country was being expatiated upon. The *role* is an important one, and has its privileges; yet, to the wolf, there is something stifling in sheep's clothing; certainly, on the occasions when it was discarded by us, a sympathy and understanding with the hotels was quickly established. Possibly they also are wolves. Undoubtedly the English tourist, with his circular ticket and his coupons, does not invariably get the best of everything. We write surrounded by him and his sufferings. An earlier visit than usual to the hotel sitting-room has revealed him, lying miserably on the sofa, shrouded in a filthy *duvet*, having been flung there at some two in the morning on his arrival, wet through, from heaven knows what tremendous walk. Subsequently we hear him being haled from his lair by the chambermaid, who treats him as the dirt under her feet (or, indeed, if we may judge by our bedroom carpet, with far less consideration).

"Here!" she says, "go in there and wash yerself!"

We hear her slamming him into a room from which two others of his kind have been recently bolted like rabbits, by the boots, to catch the 6 A.M. train. We can just faintly realise its atmosphere.

This, however, is a digression, but remotely connected with Letterbeg and Mr. Heraty's window, to which in our forlorn state we turned for distraction.

It was very small, about two feet square, but it made its appeal to all the needs of humanity from the cradle to the grave. A feeding-bottle, a rosary, a photograph of Mr. Kruger, a peg-top, a case of salmon flies, an artistic letter-weight, consisting of a pigeon's egg carved in Connemara marble, two seductively small bottles of castor-oil--these, mounted on an embankment of packets of corn-flour and rat poison, crowded the four little panes. Inside the shop the assortment ranged from bundles of reaping-hooks on the earthen floor to bottles of champagne in the murk of the top shelf. A few men leaned against the tin-covered counter, gravely drinking porter. As we stood dubiously at the door there was a padding of bare feet in the roadway, and a very small boy with a red head, dressed in a long flannel frock of a rich madder shade fluttered past us into the shop.

"Me dada says let yees be hurrying!" he gasped, between spasms of what was obviously whooping-cough. "Sweeny's case is comin' on!"

Had the message been delivered by the Sergeant-at-Arms it could not have been received with more respectful attention or been more immediately obeyed. The porter was gulped down, one unfinished glass being bestowed upon the Sergeant-at-Arms, possibly as a palliative for the whooping-cough, and the party trooped up the road towards a thatched and whitewashed cottage that stood askew at the top of a lane leading to the seashore. Two tall constables of the R.I.C. stood at the door of the cottage. It came to us, with a lifting of the heart, that we had chanced upon Petty Sessions day in Letterbeg, and this was the court-house.

It was uncommonly hot in what is called in newspapers "the body of the court". Something of the nature of a rood-screen, boarded solidly up to a height of about four feet, divided the long single room of the cottage; we, with the rest of the public, were penned in the division nearest the door. The cobwebbed boards of the loft overhead almost rested on our hats; the public, not being provided with seats by the Government, shuffled on the earthen floor and unaffectedly rested on us and each other. Within the rood-screen two magistrates sat at a table, with their suite, consisting of a clerk, an interpreter, and a district inspector of police, disposed round them.

"The young fella with the foxy mustash is Docthor Lyden," whispered an informant in response to a question, "and the owld lad that's lookin' at ye now is Heraty, that owns the shop above--"

At this juncture an emissary from the Bench very kindly offered us seats within the rood-screen. We took them, on a high wooden settle, beside the magisterial table, and the business of the court proceeded.

Close to us stood the defendant, Sweeny, a tall elderly man, with a long, composed, shaven face, and an all-observant grey eye: Irish in type, Irish in expression, intensely Irish in the self-possession in which he stood, playing to perfection the part of calm rectitude and unassailable integrity.

Facing him, the plaintiff lounged against the partition; a man strangely improbable in appearance, with close-cropped grey hair, a young, fresh-coloured face, a bristling orange moustache, and a big, blunt nose. One could have believed him a soldier, a German, anything but what he was, a peasant from the furthest shores of Western Ireland, cut off from what we call civilisation by his ignorance of any language save his own ancient speech, wherein the ideas of to-day stand out in English words like telegraph posts in a Connemara moorland.

Between the two stood the interpreter--small, old, froglike in profile, full of the dignity of the Government official.

"Well, we should be getting on now," remarked the Chairman, Heraty, J.P., after some explanatory politeness to his unexpected visitors. "William, swear the plaintiff!"

The oath was administered in Irish, and the orange moustache brushed the greasy Testament. The space above the dado of the partition became suddenly a tapestry of attentive faces, clear-eyed, all-comprehending.

"This case," announced Mr. Heraty judicially yet not without a glance at the visitors, "is a demand for compensation in the matter of a sheep that was drowned. William"--this to the interpreter--"ask Darcy what he has to say for himself?"

Darcy hitched himself round, still with a shoulder propped against the partition, and uttered, without any enthusiasm, a few nasal and guttural sentences.

"He says, yer worship," said William, with unctuous propriety, "that Sweeny's gorsoons were ever and always hunting his sheep, and settin' on their dog to hunt her, and that last week they dhrove her into the lake and dhrownded her altogether."

"Now," said Mr. Heraty, in a conversational tone, "William, when ye employ the word 'gorsoon,' do ye mean children of the male or female sex?"

"Well, yer worship," replied William, who, it may incidentally be mentioned, was himself in need of either an interpreter or of a new and complete set of teeth, "I should considher he meant ayther the one or the other."

"They're usually one or the other," said Doctor Lyden solemnly, and in a stupendous brogue. It was the first time he had spoken; he leaned back, with his hands in his pockets, and surveyed with quiet but very bright eyes the instant grin that illumined the faces of the tapestry.

"Sure William himself is no bad judge of gorsoons," said Mr. Heraty. "Hadn't he a christening in his own house three weeks ago?"

At this excursion into the family affairs of the interpreter the grin broke into a roar.

"See now, we'll ask Mr. Byrne, the schoolmaster," went on Mr. Heraty with owl-like gravity. "Isn't that Mr. Byrne that I see back there in the coort? Come forward, Mr. Byrne!"

Thus adjured, a tall, spectacled man emerged from the crowd, and, beaming with a pleasing elderly bashfulness through his spectacles, gave it as his opinion that though gorsoon was a term usually applied to the male child, it was equally applicable to the female. "But, indeed," he concluded, "the Bench has as good Irish as I have myself, and better."

"The law requires that the thransactions of this coort shall take place in English," the Chairman responded, "and we have also the public to consider."

As it was pretty certain that we were the only persons in the court who did not understand Irish, it was borne in upon us that we were the public, and we appreciated the consideration.

"We may assume, then, that the children that set on the dog wor' of both sexes," proceeded Mr. Heraty. "Well, now, as to the dog-- William, ask Darcy what sort of dog was it."

The monotonous and quiet Irish sentences followed one another again.

"That'll do. Now, William--"

"He says, yer worship, that he was a big lump of a yalla dog, an' very cross, by reason of he r'arin' a pup."

"And 'twas to make mutton-broth for the pup she dhrove Darcy's sheep in the lake, I suppose?"

A contemptuous smile passed over Darcy's face as the Chairman's sally was duly translated to him, and he made a rapid reply.

"He says there isn't one of the neighbours but got great annoyance by the same dog, yer worship, and that when the dog'd be out by night hunting, there wouldn't be a yard o' wather in the lakes but he'd have it barked over."

"It appears," observed Dr. Lyden serenely, "that the dog, like the gorsoons, was of both sexes."

"Well, well, no matther now; we'll hear what the defendant has to say. Swear Sweeny!" said Mr. Heraty, smoothing his long grey beard, with suddenly remembered judicial severity and looking menacingly over his spectacles at Sweeny. "Here, now! you don't want an interpreter! You that has a sisther married to a stationmaster and a brother in the Connaught Rangers!"

"I have as good English as anny man in this coort," said Sweeny morosely.

"Well, show it off man! What defence have ye?"

"I say that the sheep wasn't Darcy's at all," said Sweeny firmly, standing as straight as a ramrod, with his hands behind his back, a picture of surly, wronged integrity. "And there's no man livin' can prove she was. Ask him now what way did he know her?"

The question evidently touched Darcy on a tender point. He squared his big shoulders in his white flannel jacket, and turning his face for the first time towards the magistrates delivered a flood of Irish, in which we heard a word that sounded like *ullan* often repeated.

"He says, yer worships," translated William, "why wouldn't he know her! Hadn't she the *ullan* on her! He says a poor man like him would know one of the few sheep he has as well as yer worship'd know one o' yer own gowns if it had sthrayed from ye."

It is probable that we looked some of the stupefaction that we felt at this remarkable reference to Mr. Heraty's wardrobe.

"For the benefit of the general public," said Dr. Lyden, in his languid, subtle brogue, with a side-glance at that body, "it may be no harm to mention that the plaintiff is alluding to the Chairman's yearling calves and not to his costume."

"Order now!" said Mr. Heraty severely.

"An' he says," continued William, warily purging his frog-countenance of any hint of appreciation, "that Sweeny knew the *ullan* that was on her as well as himself did."

" *Ullan!* What sort of English is that for an interpreter to be using! Do ye suppose the general public knows what is an *ullan*?" interrupted Mr. Heraty with lightning rapidity. "Explain that now!"

"Why, yer worship, sure anny one in the world'd know what the *ullan* on a sheep's back is!" said William, staggered by this sudden onslaught, "though there's some might call it the *rebugh*."

"God help the Government that's payin' you wages!" said Mr. Heraty with sudden and bitter ferocity (but did we intercept a wink at his colleague?). "If it wasn't for the young family you're r'arin' in yer old age, I'd commit ye for contempt of coort!"

A frank shout of laughter, from every one in court but the victim, greeted this sally, the chorus being, as it were, barbed by a shrill crow of whooping-cough.

"Mr. Byrne!" continued Mr. Heraty without a smile, "we must call upon you again!"

Mr. Byrne's meek scholastic face once more appeared at the rood-screen.

"Well, I should say," he ventured decorously, "that the expression is locally applied to what I may call a plume or a feather that is worn on various parts of the sheep's back, for a mark, as I might say, of distinction."

"Thank you, Mr. Byrne, thank you," said Mr. Heraty, to whose imagination a vision of a plumed or feathered sheep seemed to offer nothing unusual, "remember that now, William!"

Dr. Lyden looked at his watch.

"Don't you think Sweeny might go on with his defence?" he remarked. "About the children, Sweeny--how many have ye?"

"I have four."

"And how old are they?"

"There's one o' thim is six years an another o' thim is seven--"

"Yes, and the other two eight and nine, I suppose?" commented Dr. Lyden.

The defendant remained silent.

"Do ye see now how well he began with the youngest--the way we'd think 'twas the eldest!" resumed Dr. Lyden. "I think we may assume that a gorsoon--male or female--of eight or nine years is capable of setting a dog on the sheep."

Here Darcy spoke again.

"He says," interpreted William, "there isn't pig nor ass, sheep nor duck, be-longin' to him that isn't heart-scalded with the same childhren an' their dog."

"Well, I say now, an' I swear it," said Sweeny, his eye kindling like a coal, and his voice rising as the core of what was probably an old neighbourly grudge was neared, "my land is bare from his bastes thresspassing on it, and my childhren are in dread to pass his house itself with the kicks an' the sthrokes himself an' his mother dhraws on them! The Lord Almighty knows--"

"Stop now!" said Mr. Heraty, holding up his hand. "Stop! The Lord's not inther-ferin' in this case at all! It's me an' Doctor Lyden has it to settle."

No one seemed to find anything surprising in this pronouncement; it was ac-cepted as seriously as any similar statement of the Prophet Samuel to the Children of Israel, and was evidently meant to imply that abstract justice might be expected.

"We may assume, then," said Dr. Lyden amiably, "that the sheep walked out into Sweeny's end of the lake and drowned herself there on account of the spite there was between the two families."

The court tittered. A dingy red showed itself among the grizzled hairs and wrinkles on Sweeny's cheek. In Ireland a point can often be better carried by sar-casm than by logic.

"She was blind enough to dhrown herself, or two like her!" he said angrily; "she was that owld and blind it was ayqual to her where she'd go!"

"How d'ye know she was blind?" said Mr. Heraty quickly.

"I thought the defence opened with the statement that it wasn't Darcy's sheep at all," put in Dr. Lyden, leaning back in his chair with his eyes fixed on the rafters.

Sweeny firmly regarded Mr. Heraty.

"How would I know she was blind?" he repeated. "Many's the time when she'd be takin' a sthroll in on my land I'd see her fallin' down in the rocks, she was that blind! An' didn't I see Darcy's mother one time, an' she puttin' something on her eyes."

"Was it glasses she was putting on the sheep's eyes?" suggested the Chairman, with a glance that admitted the court to the joke.

"No, but an ointment," said Sweeny stubbornly. "I seen her rubbing it to the eyes, an' she no more than thirty yards from me."

"Will ye swear that?" thundered Mr. Heraty; "will you swear that at a distance of thirty yards you could tell what was between Darcy's mother's fingers and the sheep's eyes? No you will not! Nor no man could! William, is Darcy's mother in the coort? We'll have to take evidence from her as to the condition of the sheep's eyes!"

"Darcy says, yer worship, that his mother would lose her life if she was to be brought into coort," explained William, after an interlude in Irish, to which both magistrates listened with evident interest; "that ere last night a frog jumped into the bed to her in the night, and she got out of the bed to light the Blessed Candle, and when she got back to the bed again she was in it always between herself and the wall, an' she got a wakeness out of it, and great cold--"

"Are ye sure it wasn't the frog got the wakeness?" asked Dr. Lyden.

A gale of laughter swept round the court.

"Come, come!" said Mr. Heraty; "have done with this baldherdash! William, tell Darcy some one must go fetch his mother, for as wake as she is she could walk half a mile!" Mr. Heraty here drew forth an enormous white pocket-handkerchief and trumpeted angrily in its depths.

Darcy raised his small blue eyes with their thick lashes, and took a look at his judge. There was a gabbled interchange of Irish between him and the interpreter.

"He says she could not, yer worship, nor as much as one perch."

"Ah, what nonsense is this!" said Mr. Heraty testily; "didn't I see the woman meself at Mass last Sunday?"

Darcy's reply was garnished with a good deal more gesticulation than usual, and throughout his speech the ironic smile on Sweeny's face was a masterpiece of quiet expression.

"He says," said William, "that surely she was at Mass last Sunday, the same as your worship says, but 'twas on the way home that she was taking a wall, and a stone fell on her and hurted her finger and the boot preyed on it, and it has her desthroyed."

At this culmination of the misadventures of Mrs. Darcy the countenances of the general public must; again have expressed some of the bewilderment that they felt.

"Perhaps William will be good enough to explain," said Dr. Lyden, permitting a faint smile to twitch the foxy moustache, "how Mrs. Darcy's boot affected her finger?"

William's skinny hand covered his frog mouth with all a deserving schoolboy's embarrassment at being caught out in a bad translation.

"I beg yer worships' pardon," he said, in deep confusion, "but sure your worships know as well as meself that in Irish we have the one word for your finger or your toe."

"There's one thing I know very well anyhow," said Dr. Lyden, turning to his colleague, "I've no more time to waste sitting here talking about old Kit Darcy's fingers and toes! Let the two o' them get arbitrators and settle it out of court. There's nothing between them now only the value of the sheep."

"Sure I was satisfied to leave it to arbithration, but Darcy wasn't willin'." This statement was Sweeny's.

"So you were willin' to have arbithration before you came into coort at all?" said Mr. Heraty, eyeing the tall defendant with ominous mildness. "William, ask Darcy is this the case."

Darcy's reply, delivered with a slow, sarcastic smile, provoked a laugh from the audience.

"Oh, ho! So that was the way, was it!" cried Mr. Heraty, forgetting to wait for the translation. "Ye had your wife's cousin to arbithrate! Small blame to Darcy he wasn't willin'! It's a pity ye didn't say your wife herself should arbithrate when ye went about it! You would hardly believe the high opinion Sweeny here has of his wife," continued the Chairman in illuminative excursus to Dr. Lyden; "sure he had all the women wild below at my shop th' other night sayin' his wife was the finest woman in Ireland! Upon my soul he had!"

"If I said that," growled the unfortunate Sweeny, "it was a lie for me."

"Don't ye think it might be a good thing now," suggested the indefatigable doctor, in his mournful tuneful voice, "to call a few witnesses to give evidence as to whether Mrs. Michael Sweeny is the finest woman in Ireland or no?"

"God knows, gentlemen, it's a pity ye haven't more to do this day," said Sweeny, turning at length upon his tormentors, "I'd sooner pay the price of the sheep than be losin' me time here this way."

"See, now, how we're getting to the rights of it in the latter end," commented Dr. Lyden imperturbably. "Sweeny began here by saying"--he checked off each successive point on his fingers--"that the sheep wasn't Darcy's at all. Then he said that his children of eight and nine years of age were too young to set the dog on the sheep. Then, that if the dog hunted her it was no more than she deserved for constant trespass. Then he said that the sheep was so old and blind that she committed suicide in his end of the lake in order to please herself and to spite him; and, last of all, he tells us that he offered to compensate Darcy for her before he came into court at all!"

"And on top of that," Mr. Heraty actually rose in his seat in his exquisite appreciation of the position, "on top of that, mind you, after he has the whole machinery of the law and the entire population of Letterbeg attending on him for a matter o' two hours, he informs us that we're wasting his valuable time!"

Mr. Heraty fixed his eyes in admirable passion--whether genuine or not we are quite incapable of pronouncing--upon Sweeny, who returned the gaze with all the gloom of an unfortunate but invincibly respectable man.

Dr. Lyden once more pulled out his watch.

"It might be as well for us," he said languidly, "to enter upon the inquiry as to the value of the sheep. That should take about another three-quarters of an hour. William, ask Darcy the price he puts on the sheep."

Every emotion has its limits. We received with scarce a stirring of surprise the variations of sworn testimony as to the value of the sheep. Her price ranged from one pound, claimed by Darcy and his adherents, to sixpence, at which sum her skin was unhesitatingly valued by Sweeny. Her age swung like a pendulum between two years and fourteen, and, finally, in crowning proof of her worth and general attractiveness, it was stated that her own twin had been sold for fifteen shillings to the police at Dhulish, "ere last week". At this re-entrance into the case of the personal element Mr. Heraty's spirits obviously rose.

"I think we ought to have evidence about this," he said, fixing the police officer with a dangerous eye. "Mr. Cox, have ye anny of the Dhulish police here?"

Mr. Cox, whose only official act up to the present had been the highly beneficial one of opening the window, admitted with a grin that two of the Dhulish men were in the court.

"Well, then!" continued the Chairman, "Mr. Cox, maybe ye'd kindly desire them to step forward in order that the court may be able to estimate from their appearance the nutritive qualities of the twin sisther of Darcy's sheep."

At this juncture we perceived, down near the crowded doorway, two tall and deeply embarrassed members of the R.I.C. hastily escaping into the street.

"Well, well; how easy it is to frighten the police!" remarked the Chairman, following them with a regretful eye. "I suppose, afther all, we'd betther put a price on the sheep and have done with it. In my opinion, when there's a difficulty like this--what I might call an accident--between decent men like these (for they're both decent men, and I've known them these years), I'd say both parties should share what hardship is in it. Now, doctor, what shall we give Darcy? I suppose if we gave him 8s. compensation and 2s. costs we'd not be far out?"

Dr. Lyden, already in the act of charging his pipe, nodded his head.

Sweeny began to fumble in his pockets, and drawing out a brownish rag, possibly a handkerchief, knotted in several places, proceeded to untie one of the knots. The doctor watched him without speaking. Ultimately, from some fastness in the rag a half-sovereign was extracted, and was laid upon the table by Sweeny. The clerk, a well-dressed young gentleman, whose attitude had throughout been one of the extremest aloofness, made an entry in his book with an aggressively business-like air.

"Well, that's all right," remarked Dr. Lyden, getting lazily on his legs and looking round for his hat; "it's a funny thing, but I notice that the defendant brought the exact sum required into court with him."

"I did! And I'm able to bring more than it, thanks be to God!" said Sweeny fiercely, with all the offended pride of his race. "I have two pounds here this minute--"

"If that's the way with ye, may be ye'd like us to put a bigger fine on ye!" broke in Mr. Heraty hotly, in instant response to Sweeny's show of temper.

Dr. Lyden laughed for the first time.

"Mr. Heraty's getting cross now, in the latter end," he murmured explanatorily to the general public, while he put on an overcoat, from the pocket of which protruded the Medusa coils of a stethoscope.

*   *   *   *   *

Long before the arrival of the mail-car that was to take us away, the loafers and the litigants had alike been swallowed up, apparently by the brown, hungry hillsides; possibly also, some of them, by Mr. Heraty's tap-room. Again we clambered to our places among the inevitable tourists and their inevitable bicycles, again the laden car lumbered heavily yet swiftly along the bog roads that quivered under its weight, while the water in the black ditches on either side quivered in sympathy. The tourists spoke of the vast loneliness, unconscious of the intricate network of social life that lay all around them, beyond their ken, far beyond their understanding. They spoke authoritatively of Irish affairs; mentioned that the Irish were "a bit 'ot tempered," but added that "all they wanted was fair play".

They had probably been in Ireland for a week or fortnight. They had come out of business centres in England, equipped with circular tickets, with feeling hearts, and with the belief that two and two inevitably make four; whereas in Ireland two and two are just as likely to make five, or three, and are still more likely to make nothing at all. Never will it be given to them to understand the man of whom our friend Sweeny was no more than a type. How can they be expected to realise that a man who is decorous in family and village life, indisputably God-fearing, kind to the poor, and reasonably honest, will enmesh himself in a tissue of sworn lies before his fellows for the sake of half a sovereign and a family feud, and that his fellows will think none the worse of him for it.

These things lie somewhere near the heart of the Irish problem.

THE DANE'S BREECHIN'

PART I

The story begins at the moment when my brother Robert and I had made our final arrangements for the expedition. These were considerable. Robert is a fisherman who takes himself seriously (which perhaps is fortunate, as he rarely seems to take anything else), and his paraphernalia does credit to his enthusiasm, if not to his judgment. For my part, being an amateur artist, I had strapped together a collection of painting materials that would enable me to record my inspiration in oil, watercolour, or pastel, as the spirit might move me. We had ordered a car from Coolahan's public-house in the village; an early lunch was imminent.

The latter depended upon Julia; in fact it would be difficult to mention anything at Wavecrest Cottage that did not depend on Julia. We, who were but strangers and sojourners (the cottage with the beautiful name having been lent to us, with Julia, by an Aunt), felt that our very existence hung upon her clemency. How much more then luncheon, at the revolutionary hour of a quarter to one? Even courageous people are afraid of other people's servants, and Robert and I were far from being courageous. Possibly this is why Julia treated us with compassion, even with kindness, especially Robert.

"Ah, poor Masther Robert!" I have heard her say to a friend in the kitchen, who was fortunately hard of hearing, "ye wouldn't feel him in the house no more than a feather! An' indeed, as for the two o' thim, sich gallopers never ye seen! It's hardly they'd come in the house to throw the wet boots off thim! Thim'd gallop the woods all night like the deer!"

At half-past twelve, all, as I have said, being in train, I went to the window to observe the weather, and saw a covered car with a black horse plodding along the road that separated Wavecrest Cottage from the seashore. At our modest entrance gates it drew up, and the coachman climbed from his perch with a dignity befitting his flowing grey beard and the silver band on his hat.

A covered car is a vehicle peculiar to the south of Ireland; it resembles a two-wheeled waggonette with a windowless black box on top of it. Its mouth is at the back, and it has the sinister quality of totally concealing its occupants until the ir-revocable moment when it is turned and backed against your front door steps. For this moment my brother Robert and I did not wait. A short passage and a flight of steps separated us from the kitchen; beyond the steps, and facing the kitchen door, a door opened into the garden. Robert slipped up heavily in the passage as we fled, but gained the garden door undamaged. The hall door bell pealed at my ear; I caught a glimpse of Julia, pounding chops with the rolling pin.

"Say we're out," I hissed to her--"gone out for the day! We are going into the garden!"

"Sure ye needn't give yerself that much trouble," replied Julia affably, as she snatched a grimy cap off a nail.

Nevertheless, in spite of the elasticity of Julia's conscience, the garden seemed safer.

In the garden, a plot of dense and various vegetation, decorated with Julia's lingerie, we awaited the sound of the departing wheels. But nothing departed. The breathless minutes passed, and then, through the open drawing-room window, we were aware of strange voices. The drawing-room window overlooked the garden thoroughly and commandingly. There was not a moment to lose. We plunged into the raspberry canes, and crouched beneath their embowered arches, and the fulness of the situation began to sink into our souls.

Through the window we caught a glimpse of a white beard and a portly black suit, of a black bonnet and a dolman that glittered with jet, of yet another black bonnet.

With Aunt Dora's house we had taken on, as it were, her practice, and the goodwill of her acquaintance. The Dean of Glengad and Mrs. Doherty were the very apex and flower of the latter, and in the party now installed in Aunt Dora's drawing-room I unhesitatingly recognised them, and Mrs. Doherty's sister, Miss McEvoy. Miss McEvoy was an elderly lady of the class usually described as being "not all there". The expression, I imagine, implies a regret that there should not be more. As, however, what there was of Miss McEvoy was chiefly remarkable for a monstrous appetite and a marked penchant for young men, it seems to me mainly to be regretted that there should be as much of her as there is.

A drive of nine miles in the heat of a June morning is not undertaken without a sustaining expectation of luncheon at the end of it. There were in the house three mutton chops to meet that expectation. I communicated all these facts to my brother. The consternation of his face, framed in raspberry boughs, was a picture not to be lightly forgotten. At such a moment, with everything depending on sheer nerve and resourcefulness, to consign Julia to perdition was mere self-indulgence on his part, but I suppose it was inevitable. Here the door into the garden opened and Julia came forth, with a spotless apron and a face of elaborate unconcern. She picked a handful of parsley, her black eyes questing for us among the bushes; they met mine, and a glance more alive with conspiracy it has not been my lot to receive. She moved desultorily towards us, gathering green gooseberries in her apron.

"I told them the two o' ye were out," she murmured to the gooseberry bushes. "They axed when would ye be back. I said ye went to town on the early thrain and wouldn't be back till night."

Decidedly Julia's conscience could stand alone.

"With that then," she continued, "Miss McEvoy lands into the hall, an' 'O Letitia,' says she, 'those must be the gentleman's fishing rods!' and then 'Julia!' says she, 'could ye give us a bit o' lunch?' That one's the imp!"

"Look here!" said Robert hoarsely, and with the swiftness of panic, "I'm off! I'll get out over the back wall."

At this moment Miss McEvoy put her head out of the drawing-room window and scanned the garden searchingly. Without another word we glided through the raspberry arches like departing fairies in a pantomine. The kindly lilac and laurestina bushes grew tall and thick at the end of the garden; the wall was high, but, as is usual with fruit-garden walls, it had a well-worn feasible corner that gave on to the lane leading to the village. We flung ourselves over it, and landed breathless and dishevelled, but safe, in the heart of the bed of nettles that plumed the common village ash-heap. Now that we were able, temporarily at all events, to call our souls our own, we (or rather I) took further stock of the situation. Its horrors continued to sink in. Driven from home without so much as a hat to lay our heads in, separated from those we loved most (the mutton chops, the painting materials, the fishing tackle), a promising expedition of unusual charm cut off, so to speak, in the flower of its youth--these were the more immediately obvious of the calamities which we now confronted. I preached upon them, with Cassandra eloquence, while we stood, indeterminate, among the nettles.

"And what, I ask you," I said perorating, "what on the face of the earth are we to do now?"

"Oh, it'll be all right, my dear girl," said Robert easily. Gratitude for his escape from the addresses of Miss McEvoy had apparently blinded him to the difficulties of the future. "There's Coolahan's pub. We'll get something to eat there--you'll see it'll be all right."

"But," I said, picking my way after him among the rusty tins and the broken crockery, "the Coolahans will think we're mad! We've no hats, and we can't tell them about the Dohertys."

"I don't care what they think," said Robert.

What Mrs. Coolahan may have thought, as we dived from the sunlight into her dark and porter-sodden shop, did not appear; what she looked was consternation.

"Luncheon!" she repeated with stupefaction, "luncheon! The dear help us, I have no luncheon for the like o' ye!"

"Oh, anything will do," said Robert cheerfully. His experiences at the London bar had not instructed him in the commissariat of his country.

"A bit of cold beef, or just some bread and cheese."

Mrs. Coolahan's bleared eyes rolled wildly to mine, as seeking sympathy and sanity.

"With the will o' Pether!" she exclaimed, "how would I have cold beef? And as for cheese--!" She paused, and then, curiosity over-powering all other emotions. "What ails Julia Cronelly at all that your honour's ladyship is comin' to the like o' this dirty place for your dinner?"

"Oh, Julia's run away with a soldier!" struck in Robert brilliantly.

"Small blame to her if she did itself!" said Mrs. Coolahan, gallantly accepting the jest without a change of her enormous countenance, she's a long time waiting for the chance! Maybe ourselves'd go if we were axed! I have a nice bit of salt pork in the house," she continued, "would I give your honours a rasher of it?"

Mrs. Coolahan had probably assumed that either Julia was incapably drunk, or had been dismissed without benefit of clergy; at all events she had recognised that diplomatically it was correct to change the conversation.

We adventured ourselves into the unknown recesses of the house, and sat gingerly on greasy horsehair-seated chairs, in the parlour, while the bubbling cry of the rasher and eggs arose to heaven from the frying-pan, and the reek filled the house as with a grey fog. Potent as it was, it but faintly foreshadowed the flavour of the massive slices that presently swam in briny oil on our plates. But we had breakfasted at eight; we tackled them with determination, and without too nice inspection of the three-pronged forks. We drank porter, we achieved a certain sense of satiety, that on very slight provocation would have broadened into nausea or worse. All the while the question remained in the balance as to what we were to do for our hats, and for the myriad baggage involved in the expedition.

We finally decided to write a minute inventory of what was indispensable, and to send it to Julia by the faithful hand of Mrs. Coolahan's car-driver, one Croppy, with whom previous expeditions had placed us upon intimate terms. It would be necessary to confide the position to Croppy, but this we felt, could be done without a moment's uneasiness.

By the malignity that governed all things on that troublous day, neither of us had a pencil, and Mrs. Coolahan had to be appealed to. That she had by this time properly grasped the position was apparent in the hoarse whisper in which she said, carefully closing the door after her:--

"The Dane's coachman is inside!"

Simultaneously Robert and I removed ourselves from the purview of the door.

"Don't be afraid," said our hostess reassuringly, "he'll never see ye--sure I have him safe back in the snug! Is it a writing pin ye want, Miss?" she continued, moving to the door. "Katty Ann! Bring me in the pin out o' the office!"

The Post Office was, it may be mentioned, a department of the Coolahan public-house, and was managed by a committee of the younger members of the

Coolahan family. These things are all, I believe, illegal, but they happen in Ireland. The committee was at present, apparently, in full session, judging by the flood of conversation that flowed in to us through the open door. The request for the pen caused an instant hush, followed at an interval by the slamming of drawers and other sounds of search.

"Ah, what's on ye delaying this way?" said Mrs. Coolahan irritably, advancing into the shop. "Sure I seen the pin with Helayna this morning."

At the moment all that we could see of the junior postmistress was her long bare shins, framed by the low-browed doorway, as she stood on the counter to further her researches on a top shelf.

"The Lord look down in pity on me this day!" said Mrs. Coolahan, in exalted and bitter indignation, "or on any poor creature that's striving to earn her living and has the likes o' ye to be thrusting to!"

We here attached ourselves to the outskirts of the search, which had by this time drawn into its vortex a couple of countrywomen with shawls over their heads, who had hitherto sat in decorous but observant stillness in the background. Katty Ann was rapidly examining tall bottles of sugar-stick, accustomed receptacles apparently for the pen. Helayna's raven fringe showed traces of a dive into the flour-bin. Mrs. Coolahan remained motionless in the midst, her eyes fixed on the ceiling, an exposition of suffering and of eternal remoteness from the ungodly.

We were now aware for the first time of the presence of Mr. Coolahan, a taciturn person, with a blue-black chin and a gloomy demeanour.

"Where had ye it last?" he demanded.

"I seen Katty Ann with it in the cow-house, sir," volunteered a small female Coolahan from beneath the flap of the counter.

Katty Ann, with a vindictive eye at the tell-tale, vanished.

"That the Lord Almighty might take me to Himself!" chanted Mrs. Coolahan. "Such a mee-aw! Such a thing to happen to me--the pure, decent woman! G'wout!" This, the imperative of the verb to retire, was hurtled at the tell-tale, who, presuming on her services, had incautiously left the covert of the counter, and had laid a sticky hand on her mother's skirts.

"Only that some was praying for me," pursued Mrs. Coolahan, "it might as well be the Inspector that came in the office, asking for the pin, an' if that was the way we might all go under the sod! Sich a mee-aw!"

"Musha! Musha!" breathed, prayerfully, one of the shawled women.

At this juncture I mounted on an up-ended barrel to investigate a promising lair above my head, and from this altitude was unexpectedly presented with a bird's-eye view of a hat with a silver band inside the railed and curtained "snug". I descended swiftly, not without an impression of black bottles on the snug table, and Katty Ann here slid in from the search in the cow-house.

"'Twasn't in it," she whined, "nor I didn't put it in it."

"For a pinny I'd give ye a slap in the jaw!" said Mr. Coolahan with sudden and startling ferocity.

"That the Lord Almighty might take me to Himself!" reiterated Mrs. Coolahan, while the search spread upwards through the house.

"Look here!" said Robert abruptly, "this business is going on for a week. I'm going for the things myself."

Neither I nor my remonstrances overtook him till he was well out into the street. There, outside the Coolahan door, was the Dean's inside car, resting on its shafts; while the black horse, like his driver, restored himself elsewhere beneath the Coolahan roof. Robert paid no heed to its silent warning.

"I must go myself. If I had forty pencils I couldn't explain to Julia the flies that I want!"

There comes, with the most biddable of men, a moment when argument fails, the moment of dead pull, when the creature perceives his own strength, and the astute will give in, early and imperceptibly, in order that he may not learn it beyond forgetting.

The only thing left to be done now was to accompany Robert, to avert what might be irretrievable disaster. It was now half-past one, and the three mutton chops and the stewed gooseberries must have long since yielded their uttermost to our guests. The latter would therefore have returned to the drawing-room, where it was possible that one or more of them might go to sleep. Remembering that the chops were loin-chops, we might at all events hope for some slight amount of lethargy. Again we waded through the nettles, we scaled the garden-wall, and worked our way between it and the laurestinas towards the door opposite the kitchen. There remained between us and the house an open space of about fifteen yards, fully commanded by the drawing-room window, veiling which, however, the lace curtains met in reassuring stillness. We rushed the interval, and entered the house softly. Here we were instantly met by Julia, with her mouth full, and a cup of tea in her hand. She drew us into the kitchen.

"Where are they, Julia?" I whispered. "Have they had lunch?"

"Is it lunch?" replied Julia, through bread and butter; "there isn't a bit in the house but they have it ate! And the eggs I had for the fast-day for myself, didn't That One"--I knew this to indicate Miss McEvoy--"ax an omelette from me when she seen she had no more to get!"

"Are they out of the dining-room?" broke in Robert.

"Faith, they are. 'Twas no good for them to stay in it! That One's lying up on the sofa in the dhrawing-room like any owld dog, and the Dane and Mrs. Doherty's dhrinking hot water--they have bad shtomachs, the craytures."

Robert opened the kitchen door and crept towards the dining-room, wherein, not long before the alarm, had been gathered all the essentials of the expedition. I followed him. I have never committed a burglary, but since the moment when I creaked past the drawing-room door, foretasting the instant when it would open, my sympathies are dedicated to burglars.

In two palpitating journeys we removed from the dining-room our belongings, and placed them in the kitchen; silence, fraught with dire possibilities, still brooded over the drawing-room. Could they all be asleep, or was Miss McEvoy watching us through the keyhole? There remained only my hat, which was upstairs, and at this, the last moment, Robert remembered his fly-book, left under the clock in the dining-room. I again passed the drawing-room in safety, and got upstairs, Robert effecting at the same moment his third entry into the dining-room. I was in the act of thrusting in the second hat pin when I heard the drawing-room door open. I admit that, obeying the primary instinct of self-preservation, my first impulse was to lock myself in; it passed, aided by the recollection that there was no key. I made for the landing, and from thence viewed, in a species of trance, Miss McEvoy cross-ing the hall and entering the dining-room. A long and deathly pause followed. She was a small woman; had Robert strangled her? After two or three horrible minutes a sound reached me, the well-known rattle of the side-board drawer. All then was well--Miss McEvoy was probably looking for the biscuits, and Robert must have escaped in time through the window. I took my courage in both hands and glided downstairs. As I placed my foot on the oilcloth of the hall, I was confronted by the nightmare spectacle of my brother creeping towards me on all-fours through the open door of the dining-room, and then, crowning this already over-loaded moment, there arose a series of yells from Miss McEvoy as blood-curdling as they were excusable, yet, as even in my maniac flight to the kitchen I recognised, something muffled by Marie biscuit.

It seems to me that the next incident was the composite and shattering collision of Robert, Julia and myself in the scullery doorway, followed by the swift closing of the scullery-door upon us by Julia; then the voice of the Dean of Glengad, demanding from the house at large an explanation, in a voice of cathedral severity. Miss McEvoy's reply was to us about as coherent as the shrieks of a parrot, but we plainly heard Julia murmur in the kitchen:--

"May the devil choke ye!"

Then again the Dean, this time near the kitchen door. "Julia! Where is the man who was secreted under the dinner-table?"

I gripped Robert's arm. The issues of life and death were now in Julia's hands.

"Is it who was in the dining-room, your Reverence?" asked Julia, in tones of respectful honey; "sure that was the carpenter's boy, that came to quinch a rat-hole. Sure we're destroyed with rats."

"But," pursued the Dean, raising his voice to overcome Miss McEvoy's continuous screams of explanation to Mrs. Doherty, "I understand that he left the room on his hands and knees. He must have been drunk!"

"Ah, not at all, your Reverence," replied Julia, with almost compassionate superiority, "sure that poor boy is the gentlest crayture ever came into a house. I suppose 'tis what it was he was ashamed like when Miss McEvoy comminced to screech, and faith he never stopped nor stayed till he ran out of the house like a wild goose!"

We heard the Dean reascend the kitchen steps, and make a statement of which the words "drink" and "Dora" alone reached us. The drawing-room door closed, and in the release from tension I sank heavily down upon a heap of potatoes. The wolf of laughter that had been gnawing at my vitals broke loose.

"Why did you go out of the room on your hands and knees?" I moaned, rolling in anguish on the potatoes.

"I got under the table when I heard the brute coming," said Robert, with the crossness of reaction from terror, "then she settled down to eat biscuits, and I thought I could crawl out without her seeing me"

" *Ye can come out*!" said Julia's mouth, appearing at a crack of the scullery door, "I have as many lies told for ye--God forgive me!--as'd bog a noddy!"

This mysterious contingency might have impressed us more had the artist been able to conceal her legitimate pride in her handiwork. We emerged from the chill and varied smells of the scullery, retaining just sufficient social self-control to keep us from flinging ourselves with grateful tears upon Julia's neck. Shaken as we were, the expedition still lay open before us; the game was in our hands. We were winning by tricks, and Julia held all the honours.

PART II

Perhaps it was the clinging memory of the fried pork, perhaps it was because all my favourite brushes were standing in a mug of soft soap on my washing stand, or because Robert had in his flight forgotten to replenish his cigarette case, but there was no doubt but that the expedition languished.

There was no fault to be found with the setting. The pool in which the river coiled itself under the pine-trees was black and brimming, the fish were rising at the flies that wrought above it, like a spotted net veil in hysterics, the distant hills lay in sleepy undulations of every shade of blue, the grass was warm, and not unduly peopled with ants. But some impalpable blight was upon us. I ranged like a lost soul along the banks of the river--a lost soul that is condemned to bear a burden of some two stone of sketching materials, and a sketching umbrella with a defective joint--in search of a point of view that for ever eluded me. Robert cast his choicest flies, with delicate quiverings, with coquettish withdrawals; had they been cannon-balls they could hardly have had a more intimidating effect upon the trout. Where Robert fished a Sabbath stillness reigned, beyond that charmed area they rose like notes of exclamation in a French novel. I was on the whole inclined to trace these things back to the influence of the pork, working on systems weakened by shock; but Robert was not in the mood to trace them to anything. Unsuccessful fishermen are not fond of introspective suggestions. The member of the expedition who enjoyed himself beyond any question was Mrs. Coolahan's car-horse. Having been taken out of the shafts on the road above the river, he had with his harness on his back, like Horatius, unhesitatingly lumbered over a respectable bank and ditch in the wake of Croppy, who had preceded him with the reins. He was now grazing luxuriously along the river's edge, while his driver smoked, no less luxuriously, in the background.

"Will I carry the box for ye, Miss?" Croppy inquired compassionately, stuffing his lighted pipe into his pocket, as I drifted desolately past him. "Sure you're killed with the load you have! This is a rough owld place for a lady to be walkin'. Sit down, Miss. God knows you have a right to be tired."

It seemed that with Croppy also the day was dragging, doubtless he too had lunched on Mrs. Coolahan's pork. He planted my camp-stool and I sank upon it.

"Well, now, for all it's so throublesome," he resumed, "I'd say painting was a nice thrade. There was a gintleman here one time that was a painther--I used to be dhrivin' him. Faith! there wasn't a place in the counthry but he had it pathrolled. He seen me mother one day--cleaning fish, I b'lieve she was, below on the quay--an' nothing would howld him but he should dhraw out her picture!" Croppy laughed unfilially. "Well, me mother was mad. 'To the divil I pitch him!' says she; 'if I wants me photograph drew out I'm liable to pay for it,' says she, 'an' not to be stuck up before the ginthry to be ped for the like o' that!' 'Tis for; you bein' so handsome!' says I to her. She was black mad altogether then. 'If that's the way,' says she, 'it's a wondher he wouldn't ax yerself, ye rotten little rat,' says she, 'in place of thrying could he make a show of yer poor little ugly little cock-nosed mother!' 'Faith!' says I to her, 'I wouldn't care if the divil himself axed it, if he give me a half-crown and nothing to do but to be sittin' down!'"

The tale may or may not have been intended to have a personal application, but Croppy's fat scarlet face and yellow moustache, bristling beneath a nose which he must have inherited from his mother, did not lend themselves to a landscape background, and I fell to fugitive pencil sketches of the old white car-horse as he grazed round us. It was thus that I first came to notice a fact whose bearing upon our fortunes I was far from suspecting. The old horse's harness was of dingy brown leather, with dingier brass mountings; it had been frequently mended, in varying shades of brown, and, in remarkable contrast to the rest of the outfit, the breeching was of solid and well-polished black leather, with silver buckles. It was not so much the discrepancy of the breeching as its respectability that jarred upon me; finally I commented upon it to Croppy.

His cap was tilted over the maternal nose, he glanced at me sideways from under its peak.

"Sure the other breechin' was broke, and if that owld shkin was to go the lin'th of himself without a breechin' on him he'd break all before him! There was some fellas took him to a funeral one time without a breechin' on him, an' when he seen the hearse what did he do but to rise up in the sky."

Wherein lay the moral support of a breeching in such a contingency it is hard to say. I accepted the fact without comment, and expressed a regret that we had not been indulged with the entire set of black harness.

Croppy measured me with his eye, grinned bashfully, and said:--

"Sure it's the Dane's breechin' we have, Miss! I daresay he'd hardly get home at all if we took any more from him!"

The Dean's breeching! For an instant a wild confusion of ideas deprived me of the power of speech. I could only hope that Croppy had left him his gaiters! Then I pulled myself together.

"Croppy," I said in consternation, "how did you get it? Did you borrow it from the coachman?"

"Is it the coachman!" said Croppy tranquilly. "I did not, Miss. Sure he was asleep in the snug."

"But can they get home without it?"

A sudden alarm chilled me to the marrow.

"Arrah, why not, Miss? That black horse of the Dane's wouldn't care if there was nothing at all on him!"

I heard Robert reeling in his line--had he a fish? Or, better still, had he made up his mind to go home?

As a matter of fact, neither was the case; Robert was merely fractious, and in that particular mood when he wished to have his mind imperceptibly made up for him, while prepared to combat any direct suggestion. From what quarter the ignoble proposition that we should go home arose is immaterial. It is enough to say that Robert believed it to be his own, and that, before he had time to reconsider the question, the tactful Croppy had crammed the old white horse into the shafts of the car.

It was by this time past five o'clock, and a threatening range of clouds was rising from seaward across the west. Things had been against us from the first, and if the last stone in the sling of Fate was that we were to be wet through before we got home, it would be no more than I expected. The old horse, however, addressed himself to the eight Irish miles that lay between him and home with unexpected vivacity. We swung in the ruts, we shook like jellies on the merciless patches of broken stones, and Croppy stimulated the pace with weird whistlings through his teeth, and heavy prods with the butt of his whip in the region of the borrowed breeching.

Now that the expedition had been shaken off and cast behind us, the humbler possibilities of the day began to stretch out alluring hands. There was the new box from the library; there was the afternoon post; there was a belated tea, with a peaceful fatigue to endear all. We reached at last the welcome turn that brought us into the coast road. We were but three miles now from that happy home from which we had been driven forth, years ago as it seemed, at such desperate hazard. We drove pleasantly along the road at the top of the cliffs. The wind was behind us; a rising tide plunged and splashed far below. It was already raining a little, enough to justify our sagacity in leaving the river, enough to lend a touch of passion to the thought of home and Julia.

The grey horse began to lean back against the borrowed breeching, the chains of the traces clanked loosely. We had begun the long zig-zag slant down to the village. We swung gallantly round the sharp turn half-way down the hill.

And there, not fifty yards away, was the Dean's inside car, labouring slowly, inevitably, up to meet us. Even in that stupefying moment I was aware that the silver-banded hat was at a most uncanonical angle. Behind me on the car was stowed my sketching umbrella; I tore it from the retaining embrace of the camp-stool, and unfurled its unwieldy tent with a speed that I have never since achieved. Robert, on the far side of the car, was reasonably safe. The inestimable Croppy quickened up. Cowering beneath the umbrella, I awaited the crucial moment at which to shift its protection from the side to the back. The sound of the approaching wheels told me that it had almost arrived, and then, suddenly, without a note of warning, there came a scurry of hoofs, a grinding of wheels, and a confused outcry of voices. A violent jerk nearly pitched me off the car, as Croppy dragged the white horse into the opposite bank; the umbrella flew from my hand and revealed to me the Dean's bearded coachman sitting on the road scarcely a yard from my feet, uttering large and drunken shouts, while the covered car hurried back towards the village with the unforgettable yell of Miss McEvoy bursting from its curtained rear. The black horse was not absolutely running away, but he was obviously alarmed, and with the long hill before him anything might happen.

"They're dead! They're dead!" said Croppy, with philosophic calm; "'twas the parasol started him."

As he spoke, the black horse stumbled, the laden car ran on top of him like a landslip, and, with an abortive flounder, he collapsed beneath it. Once down, he lay, after the manner of his kind, like a dead thing, and the covered car, propped on its shafts, presented its open mouth to the heavens. Even as I sped headlong to the rescue in the wake of Robert and Croppy, I fore-knew that Fate had after all been too many for us, and when, an instant later, I seated myself in the orthodox manner upon the black horse's winker, and perceived that one of the shafts was broken, I was already, in spirit, making up beds with Julia for the reception of the party.

To this mental picture the howls of Miss McEvoy during the process of extraction from the covered car lent a pleasing reality.

Only those who have been in a covered car under similar circumstances can at all appreciate the difficulty of getting out of it. It has once, in the streets of Cork, happened to me, and I can best compare it to escaping from the cabin of a yacht without the aid of a companion ladder. From Robert I can only collect the facts that the door jammed, and that, at a critical juncture, Miss McEvoy had put her arms round his neck.

*　　*　　*　　*　　*

The programme that Fate had ordained was carried out to its ultimate item. The party from the Deanery of Glengad spent the night at Wavecrest Cottage, attired by subscription, like the converts of a Mission; I spent it in the attic, among trunks of Aunt Dora's old clothes, and rats; Robert, who throughout had played an unworthy part, in the night mail to Dublin, called away for twenty-four hours on a pretext that would not have deceived an infant a week old.

Croppy was firm and circumstantial in laying the blame on me and the sketching umbrella.

"Sure, I seen the horse wondhering at it an' he comin' up the hill to us. 'Twas that turned him."

The dissertation in which the Dean's venerable coachman made the entire disaster hinge upon the theft of the breeching was able, but cannot conveniently be here set down.

For my part, I hold with Julia.

"'Twas Helayna gave the dhrink to the Dane's coachman! The low cursed thing! There isn't another one in the place that'd do it! I'm told the priest was near breaking his umbrella on her over it."

"MATCHBOX"

It was the event of Mr. John Denny's life that he valued highest. It is twenty years now since it took place, and many other things have happened to him, such as going to England to give evidence in the Parnell Commission, and matrimony, and taking the second prize in the Lightweight Hunter Class at the Dublin Horse Show. But none of them, not even the trip to London, possesses quite the same fortunate blend of the sublime and the ridiculous that gives this incident such a perennial success at the Hunt and Agricultural Show dinners which are the dazzling breaks in the monotony of Mr. Denny's life, and he prized it accordingly.

Mr. Johnny Denny--or Dinny Johnny as he was known to his wittier friends-- was a young man of the straightest sect of the Cork buckeens, a body whose importance justifies perhaps a particular description of one of their number. His profession was something imperceptibly connected with the County Grand Jury Office, and was quite over-shadowed in winter by the gravities of hunting, and in summer by the gallantries of the Militia training; for, like many of his class, he was a captain in the Militia. He was always neatly dressed; his large moustache looked as if it shared with his boots the attention of the blacking brush. No cavalry sergeant in Ballincollig had a more delicately bowed leg, nor any creature, except, perhaps, a fox-terrier interviewing a rival, a more consummate swagger. He knew every horse and groom in all the leading livery stables, and, in moments of expansion, would volunteer to name the price at which any given animal could be safeguarded from any given veterinary criticism. With all these not specially attractive qualities, however, Dinny Johnny was, and is, a good fellow in his way. His temper was excellent, his courage indisputable; he has never been known to give any horse--not even a hireling--less than fair play, and a tendency to ride too close to hounds has waned since time, like an Irish elector, has taken to emphasising himself by throwing stones, and Dinny

Johnny, once ten stone, now admits to riding 13.7.

In those days, before the inertia that creeps like mildew over country house-holders had begun to form, Mr. Denny was in the habit of making occasional excursions into remote parts of the County Cork in search of those flowers of pony perfection that are supposed to blush unseen in any sufficiently mountainous and unknown country, and the belief in which is the touch of wild poetry that keeps alive the soul of the amateur horse coper. He had never met the pony of his dreams, but he had not lost faith in it, and though he would range through the Bantry fair with a sour eye, behind the sourness there was ever a kindling spark of hope.

Towards the end of October, in the year '83, Mr. Denny received an invitation from an old friend to go down to "the West"--thus are those regions east of the moon, and west of the sun, and south-west of Drimoleague Junction, designated in the tongue of Cork civilisation--to "look at a colt," and with a saddle and bridle in the netting and a tooth-brush in his pocket he set his face for the wilderness. I have no time to linger over the circumstances of the deal. Suffice it to say that, after an arduous haggle, Mr. Denny bought the colt, and set forth the same day to ride him by easy stages to his future home.

It was a wet day, wet with the solid determination of a western day, and the loaded clouds were flinging their burden down on the furze, and the rocks, and the steep, narrow road, with vindictive ecstacy. They also flung it upon Mr. Denny, and both he and his new purchase were glad to find a temporary shelter in one of the many public-houses of a village on the line of march. He was sitting warming himself at an indifferent turf fire, and drinking a tumbler of hot punch, when the sound of loud voices outside drew him to the window. In front of a semi-circle of blue frieze coats, brown frieze trousers and slouched black felt hats, stood a dejected grey pony, with a woman at its head and a lanky young man on its back; and it was obvious to Mr. Denny that a transaction, of an even more fervid sort than that in which he had recently engaged, was toward.

"Fifteen pound!" screamed the woman, darting a black head on the end of a skinny neck out of the projecting hood of her cloak with the swiftness of a lizard; "fifteen pound, James Hallahane, and the divil burn the ha'penny less that I'll take for her!"

The elderly man to whom this was addressed continued to gaze steadily at the ground, and turning his head slightly away, spat unostentatiously. The other men moved a little, vaguely, and one said in a tone of remote soliloquy:--

"She wouldn't go tin pound in Banthry fair."

"Tin pound!" echoed the pony's owner shrilly. "Ah, God help ye, poor man! Here, Patsey, away home wid ye out o' this. It'll be night, and dark night itself before--"

"I'll give ye eleven pounds," said James Hallahane, addressing the toes of his boots. The young man on the pony turned a questioning eye towards his mother, but her sole response was a drag at the pony's head to set it going; swinging her cloak about her, she paddled through the slush towards the gate, supremely disregarding the fact that a gander, having nerved himself and his harem to the charge, had caught the ragged skirt of her dress in his beak, and being too angry to let go, was being whirled out of the yard in her train.

Dinny Johnny ran to the door, moved by an impulse for which I think the hot whisky and water must have been responsible.

"I'll give you twelve pounds for the pony, ma'am!" he called out.

A quarter of an hour later, when he and the publican were tying a tow-rope round the pony's lean neck, Mr. Denny was aware of a sinking of the heart as he surveyed his bargain. It looked, and was, an utterly degraded little object, as it stood with its tail tucked in between its drooping hindquarters, and the rain running in brown streams down its legs. Its lips were decorated with the absurd, the almost incredible moustache that is the consequence among Irish horses of a furze diet (I would hesitatingly direct the attention of the male youth of Britain to this singular but undoubted fact), and although the hot whisky and water had not exaggerated the excellence of its shoulder and the iron soundness of its legs, it had certainly reversed the curve of its neck and levelled the corrugations of its ribs.

"You could strike a bally match on her, this minute, if it wasn't so wet!" thought Mr. Denny, and with the simple humour that endeared him to his friends he christened the pony "Matchbox" on the spot.

"And it's to make a hunther of her ye'd do?" said the publican, pulling hard at the knot of the tow-rope. "Begor', I know that one. If there was forty men and their wives, and they after her wid sticks, she wouldn't lep a sod o' turf. Well, safe home, sir, safe home, and mind out she wouldn't kick ye. She's a cross thief," and with this valediction Dinny Johnny went on his way.

There was no disputing the fact of the pony's crossness.

"She's sourish-like in her timper," Jimmy, Mr. Denny's head man, observed to his subordinate not long after the arrival, and the subordinate, tenderly stroking a bruised knee, replied:--

"Sour! I niver see the like of her! Be gannies, the divil's always busy with her!"

On one point, however, the grey pony proved better than had been anticipated. Without the intervention of the forty married couples she took to jumping at once.

"It comes as aisy to her as lies to a tinker," said Jimmy to a criticising friend; "the first day ever I had her out on a string she wint up to the big bounds fence between us and Barrett's as indipindant as if she was going to her bed; and she jumped it as flippant and as crabbed--By dam, she's as crabbed as a monkey!"

In those days Mr. Standish O'Grady, popularly known as "Owld Sta'," had the hounds, and it need scarcely be said that Mr. Denny was one of his most faithful followers. This season he had not done as well as usual. The colt was only turning out moderately, and though the pony was undoubtedly both crabbed and flippant, she could not be expected to do much with nearly twelve stone on her back. It happened, therefore, that Mr. Denny took his pleasure a little sadly, with his loins girded in momentary expectation of trouble, and of a sudden refusal from the colt to jump until the crowd of skirters and gap-hunters drew round, and escape was impossible until Mrs. Tom Graves's splinty old carriage horse had ploughed its way through the bank, and all those whom he most contemned had flaunted through the breach in front of him. He rode the pony now and then, but he more often lent her to little Mary O'Grady, "Owld Sta's" untidy, red-cheeked, blue-eyed, and quite uneducated little girl. It was probable that Mary could only just write her name, and it was obvious that she could not do her hair; but she was afraid of nothing that went on four legs--in Ireland, at least--and she had the divine gift of "hands". From the time when she was five, up till now, when she was fifteen, Mr. Denny had been her particular adherent, and now he found a chastened pleasure in having his eye wiped by Mary, on the grey pony; moreover, experience showed him that if anything would persuade the colt to jump freely, it was getting a lead from the little mare.

"Upon my soul, she wasn't such a bad bargain after all," he thought one pleasant December day as he jogged to the Meet, leading "Matchbox," who was fidgeting along beside him with an expression of such shrewishness as can only be assumed by a pony mare; "if it wasn't that Mary likes riding her I'd make her up a bit and she'd bring thirty-five anywhere."

There had been, that autumn, a good deal of what was euphemistically described as "trouble" in that district of the County Cork which Mr. Denny and the Kilcronan hounds graced with their society, and when Mr. O'Grady and his field assembled at the Curragh-coolaghy cross-roads, it was darkly hinted that if the hounds ran over a certain farm not far from the covert, there might be more trouble.

Dinny Johnny, occupied with pulling up Mary O'Grady's saddle girths, and evading the snaps with which "Matchbox" acknowledged the attention, thought little of these rumours.

"Nonsense!" he said; "whatever they do they'll let the hounds alone. Come on, Mary, you and me'll sneak down to the north side of the wood. He's bound to break there, and we've got to take every chance we can get."

Curragh-coolaghy covert was a large, ill-kept plantation that straggled over a long hillside fighting with furze-bushes and rocks for the right of possession; a place wherein the young hounds could catch and eat rabbits to their heart's content comfortably aware that the net of brambles that stretched from tree to tree would effectually screen them from punishment. From its north-east side a fairly smooth country trended down to a river, and if the fox did not fulfil Mr. Denny's expectations by breaking to the north, the purplish patch that showed where, on the further side of the river, Madore Wood lay, looked a point for which he would be likely to make. Conscious of an act which he would have loudly condemned in any one else, Mr. Denny, followed by Mary, like his shadow, rode quietly round the long flank of the covert to the north-east corner. They sat in perfect stillness for a few minutes, and then there came a rustling on the inside of the high, bracken-fringed fence which divided them from the covert. Then a countryman's voice said in a cautious whisper:--

"Did he put in the hounds yit?"

"He did," said another voice, "he put them in the soud-aisht side; they'll be apt to get it soon."

"Get what?" thought Dinny Johnny, all his bristles rising in wrath as the idea of a drag came to him.

"There! they're noising now!" said the first voice, while a whimper or two came from far back in the wood. "Maybe there'll not be so much chat out o' thim afther once they'll git to Madore!"

"'Twas a pity Scanlan wouldn't put the mate in here and have done with it," said the second voice. "Owld Sta'll niver let them run a dhrag."

"Yirrah, what dhrag man! 'Twas the fox himself they had, and he cut open to make a good thrail, and the way Scanlan laid it the devil himself wouldn't know 'twas a dhrag, and they have little Danny Casey below to screech he seen the fox--"

At the same instant the whimpers swelled into a far-away chorus, that grew each moment fainter and more faint. Much as Mr. Denny desired to undertake the capture of the imparters of these interesting facts, he knew that he had now no time to attempt it, and, with a shout to Mary, he started the colt at full gallop up the rough hillside, round the covert, while the grey pony scuttled after him as nimbly as a rabbit. The colt seemed to realise the stress of the occasion, and jumped steadily enough; but the last fence on to the road was too much for his nerves, and, having swerved from it with discomposing abruptness, he fell to his wonted tactics of rearing and backing.

Mr. Denny permitted himself one minute in which to establish the fruitlessness of spurs, whip and blasphemy in this emergency, and then, descending to his own legs, he climbed over the fence into the road and ran as fast as boots and tops would let him towards the point whence the cry of the hounds was coming, ever more and more faintly. In a moment or two he returned, out of breath, to where the faithful Mary awaited him.

"It's no good, Mary," he said, wiping the perspiration from his forehead; "they're running like blazes to the south along through the furze. I suppose the devils took it that way to humbug your father, and then they'll turn for the bridge and run into Madore; and there's the end of the hounds."

Mary, who regarded the hounds as the chief, if not the only, object of existence, looked at him with scared eyes, while the colour died out of her round cheeks.

"Will they be poisoned, Mr. Denny?" she gasped.

"Every man jack of them, if your father doesn't twig it's a drag, and whip 'em off," replied Mr. Denny, with grim brevity.

"Couldn't we catch them up?" cried Mary, almost incoherent from excitement and horror.

"They've gone half-a-mile by this, and that brute," this with an eye of concentrated hatred at the colt, "won't jump a broom-stick."

"But let me try," urged Mary, maddened by the assumption of masculine calm which Mr. Denny's despair had taken on; "or--oh, Mr. Denny, if you rode 'Matchbox' yourself straight to Madore across the river, you'd be in time to whip them off!"

"By Jove!" said Dinny Johnny, and was silent. I believe that was the moment at which the identity of the future Mrs. Denny was made clear to him.

"And you'll have to ride her in my saddle!" went on Mary at lightning speed, taking control of the situation in a manner prophetic of her future successful career as a matron. "There isn't time to change--"

"The devil I shall!" said Dinny Johnny, and an unworthy thought of what his friends would say flitted across his mind.

"And you'll have to sit sideways, because the lowest crutch is so far back there's not room for your leg if you sit saddleways," continued his preceptor breathlessly. "I know it--Jimmy said so when he rode her to the meet for me last week. Oh hurry--hurry! How slow you are!"

Mr. Denny never quite knew how he got into the horrors of the saddle, still less how he and "Matchbox" got into the road. At one acute moment, indeed, he had believed he was going to precede her thither, but they alighted more or less together, and turning her, by a handy gap, into the field on the other side of the road, he set off at a precarious gallop, followed by the encouraging shrieks of Mary.

"Thank the Lord there's no one looking, and it's a decent old saddle with a pommel on the offside," he said to himself piously, while he grasped the curving snout of the pommel in question, "I'd be a dead man this minute only for that."

He felt as though he were wedged in among the claws of a giant crab, but without the sense of retention that might be hoped for under such circumstances. The lowest crutch held one leg in aching durance; there was but just room for the other between the two upper horns, and the saddle was so short and hollow in the seat that its high-ridged cantle was the only portion from which he derived any support--a support that was suddenly and painfully experienced after each jump. He could see, very far off, the pink coat of "Owld Sta'" following a line which seemed each moment to be turning more directly for Madore, and in his agony he gave the pony an imprudent dig of the spur that sent her on and off a boggy fence in two goat-like bounds, and gave the sunlight opportunity to play intermittently upon the hollow seat of the saddle. She had never carried him so well, and as she put her little head down and raced at the fences, the unfortunate Dinny Johnny felt that though he was probably going to break his neck, no one would ever be able to mention his early demise without a grin.

Field after field fled by him in painful succession till he found himself safe on the farther side of a big stone-faced "double," the last fence before the river.

"Please God I'll never be a woman again!" ejaculated Mr. Denny as he wedged his left leg more tightly in behind the torturing leaping horn, "that was a hairy old place! I wish Mary saw the pair of us coming up on to it like new-born stags!"

Had Mary seen him and "Matchbox" a moment later, emerging separately from a hole in mid stream, her respect might not have prevented her from laughing, but the fact remains that the pair got across somehow. At the top of the hill beyond the river Dinny Johnny saw the hounds for the first time. They had checked on the road by the bridge, but now he heard them throwing their tongues as they hit the line again, the fatal line that was leading them to the covert. Even at this moment, Mr. Denny could not restrain an admiration that would appear to most people ill-timed.

"Aren't they going the hell of a docket!" he exclaimed fondly, "and good old Chantress leading the lot of them, the darling! It'll be a queer thing now, if I don't get there in time!"

Blown though the pony was, he knew instinctively that he had not yet come to the end of her, and he drove her along at a canter until he reached a lane that encircled the covert, along which he would have to go to intercept the hounds. As he jumped into it he was suddenly aware of a yelling crowd of men and boys, who seemed, with nightmare unexpectedness, to fill all the lane behind him. He knew what they were there for, and oblivious of the lamentable absurdity of his appearance, he turned and roared out a defiance as he clattered at full speed down the stony lane. It seemed like another and almost expected episode in the nightmare when he became aware of a barricade of stones, built across the road to a height of about four feet, with along the top of it--raising it to what, on a fourteen hand pony, looked like impossibility--the branch of a fir-tree, with all its bristling twigs left on it.

He heard the cry of the hounds clearly now; they were within a couple of fields of the covert. Dinny Johnny drove his left spur into the little mare's panting side, let go the crutch, took hold of her head in the way that is unmistakable, and faced her at the barricade. As he did so a countryman sprang up at his right hand and struck furiously at him with a heavy potato spade. The blow was aimed at Dinny Johnny, but the moment was miscalculated, and it fell on "Matchbox" instead. The sharp blade gashed her hind quarter, but with a spring like a frightened deer she rose to the jump. For one supreme moment Dinny Johnny thought she had cleared it, but at the next her hind legs had caught in the branch, and with a jerk that sent her rider flying over her head, she fell in a heap on the road. Fortunately for Mr. Denny, he was a proficient in the art of falling, and though his hands were cut, and blood was streaming down his face, he was able to struggle up, and run on towards the cry of the hounds. There was still time; panting and dizzy, and half-blinded with his own blood, he knew that there was still time, and he laboured on, heedless of everything but the hounds. A high wall divided the covert from the lane, and he could see the gate that was the sole entrance to the wood on this side standing open. It was an iron gate, very high, with close upright iron bars and Chantress was racing him to get there first, Chantress, with all the pack at her heels.

*   *   *   *   *

Dinny Johnny won. It was a very close thing between him and Chantress, and that good hound's valuable nose came near being caught as the gates clanged together, but Dinny Johnny was in first. Then he flung himself at the pack, whipping, slashing, and swearing like a madman, as indeed he was for the moment. He had often whipped for Mr. O'Grady, and the hounds knew him, but without the solid abetting of the wall and the gate, he would have had but a poor chance. As it was, he whipped them back into the field up which they had run, and as he did so, "Owld

Sta'" came puffing up the hill, with about a dozen of the field hard at his heels.

"Poison!" gasped Dinny Johnny, falling down at full length on the grass, "the wood's poisoned!"

When they went back to look for "Matchbox" she was still lying in the bohireen. Her bridle had vanished, and so had the pursuing countrymen. Mary O'Grady's saddle was broken, and could never be used again, and no more could "Matchbox," because she had broken her neck.

And so the hounds, whom she had saved, subsequently ate her; but one of her little hoofs commemorates her name, and as Mr. Denny, with its assistance, lights his after-dinner pipe, he often heaves an appropriate sigh, and remarks: "Well, Mary, we'll never get the like of that pony again".

"AS I WAS GOING TO BANDON FAIR"

The first glimpse was worthy the best traditions of an Irish horse-fair. The train moved slowly across a bridge; beneath it lay the principal street of Bandon, seething with horses, loud with voices, and as the engine-driver, with the stern humour of his kind, let loose the usual assortment of sounds, it seemed as though the roadway below boiled over. Horses reared, plunged and stampeded, while high above the head of a long-tailed chestnut a countryman floated forth into space, a vision, in its brief perfectness, delightfully photographed on the retina.

From the moment of leaving the railway station the fair was all pervading. It appeared that the whole district had turned horse dealer. The cramped side pavements of the town failed to accommodate the ceaseless promenade of those whose sole business lay in criticising the companion promenade of horses in the narrow street. They haled horses before them with the aplomb of a colonel of cavalry buying remounts.

"Hi! bay horse! Pull in here! Foxy mare! Hi, boy, bring up that foxy mare!"

The ensuing comments, though mainly of a damaging nature, were understood on both sides to be no more than conventional dismissals. The bay horse and the foxy mare were re-absorbed in the stream; their critics directed their attentions elsewhere with unquenched assiduity.

It is the truest, most changeless trait of Irish character, the desire to stand well with the horse, to be his confidant, his physician, his exponent. It is comparable to the inborn persuasion in the heart of every man that he is a judge of wine.

The procession of horses in the long, narrow street makes the brain swim. Hardly has the eye taken in the elderly and astute hunter with the fired hocks, whose forelegs look best in action, when it is dazzled by the career of a cart-horse, scourged to a mighty canter by a boy with a rope's end, or it is horrified by the hair-breadth escape of a group of hooded countrywomen from before the neighing charge of a two-year-old in a halter and string. Yet these things are the mere preliminary to the fair. At the end of the town a gap broken in a fence admits to a long field on a hillside. The entrance is perilous, and before it is achieved may involve more than one headlong flight to the safe summit of a friendly wall, as the young horses protest, and whirl, and buck with the usual fatuity of their kind. Once within the fair field there befal the enticements of the green apple, of the dark-complexioned sweetmeat temptingly denominated "Peggy's leg," of the "crackers"--that is, a confection resembling dog biscuit sown with caraway seeds--and, above all, of the "crubeens," which, being interpreted, means "pigs' feet," slightly salted, boiled, cold, wholly abominable. Here also is the three-card trick, demonstrated by a man with the incongruous accent of Whitechapel and a defiant eye, that even through the glaze of the second stage of drunkenness held the audience and yet was 'ware of the disposition of the nine of hearts. Here is the drinking booth, and here sundry itinerant vendors of old clothes, and--of all improbable commodities to be found at a horse-fair--wall-paper. Neither has much success. The old-clothes woman casts down a heap of singularly repellant rags before a disparaging customer; she beats them with her fists, presumably to show their soundness in wind and limb: a cloud of germ-laden dust arises.

"Arrah!" she says; "the divil himself wouldn't plaze ye in clothes."

The wall-paper man is not more fortunate. "Look at that for a nate patthern!" he says ecstatically, "that'd paper a bed! Come now, ma'am, wan an' thrippence!"

The would-be purchaser silently tests it with a wrinkled finger and thumb, and shakes her head.

"Well, I declare to ye now, that's a grand paper. If ye papered a room with that and put a hen in it she'd lay four eggs!" But not even the consideration of its value as an aesthetic stimulant can compass the sale of the one-and-threepenny wall-paper.

Down at this end of the fair field congregate the three-year-olds and two-year-olds; they pierce the air with their infant squeals and neighs, they stamp, and glare, and strike attitudes with absurd statuesqueness, while their owners sit on a bank above them, playing them like fish on the end of a long rope, and fabling forth their perfections with tireless fancy. The perils of the way increase at every moment. In and out among the restless heels the onlooker must steer his course, up into the ampler space on the hill-top, where the horses stand in more open order and a general view is possible.

Much may be learned at Bandon Fair of how the County Cork hunter is arrived at, of the Lord Hastings colt out of a high-bred Victor mare; of New Laund, of Speculation, of Whalebone, of the ancient and well-nigh mythical Druid, whose name adds a lustre to any pedigree. These things are matters far more real and serious than English history to every man and boy in the fair field, whether he is concerned in practical horse-dealing or not. Even the mere visitor is fired with the acquisition of knowledge, and, in the intervals of saving his life, casts a withering eye on hocks and forelegs, and cultivates the gloomy silence that distinguishes the buyer.

It can hardly fail to attract the attention of the inquirer that, in the highest walks of horsiness, the desire to appear horsey has been left behind. These shining ones have passed beyond symbols of canes, of gaiters, of straws in the mouth; it is as though they craved that incognito which for them is for ever impossible. Bandon Fair was privileged to have drawn two such into its shouting vortex. One wears a simple suit of black serge, with trousers of a godly fulness; in it he might fitly hand round the plate in church. His manner is almost startlingly candid, his speech, what there is of it, is ungarnished with stable slang, his face might belong to an imperfectly shaved archbishop. Yesterday he bought twenty young horses; next week he will buy forty more; next year he will place them in the English shires at prices never heard of in Bandon, and, be it added, they will as a rule be worth the money. Here is another noted judge of horseflesh, in knickerbocker breeches that seem to have been made at home for some one else, in leather gaiters of unostentatious roominess and rusticity. Though the August day is innocent of all suggestion of rain, he carries instead of a riding cane a matronly umbrella. When he rides a horse, and he rides several with a singularly intimate and finished method, he hands the umbrella to a reverential bystander; when the trial is over the umbrella is reassumed. If anything were needed to accent its artless domesticity, it would be the group of boys, horse copers in ambition, possibly in achievement, who sit in a row under a fence, with their teeth grimly clenched upon clay pipes, their eyes screwed up in perpetual and ungenial observation. Their conversation is telegraphic, smileless, esoteric, and punctuated with expectoration. If Phaeton and the horses of the sun were to take a turn round the fair field these critics would find little in them to commend. They are in the primary phase of a life-long art; perhaps with time and exceptional favours of fortune it may be given to them to learn the disarming mildness, the simplicity, that, like a water-lily, is the perfected outcome of the deep.

Before two o'clock the magnates of the fair had left it, taking with them the cream of its contents, and in humbler people such a hunger began to assert itself as came near bringing even crubeens and Peggy's leg within the sphere of practical politics. While slowly struggling through the swarming street the perfume of mutton chops stole exquisitely forth from the door of one of the hotels, accompanied by the sound of a subdued fusillade of soda-water corks; over the heads of the filthy press of people round the entrance and the thirsty throng at the bar might be seen a procession of gaitered legs going upstairs to luncheon. It seemed an excellent idea. The air within was blue with tobacco smoke, flushed henchwomen staggered to and fro with arms spread wide across trays of whiskies and sodas, opening doors revealed rooms full of men, mutton chops and mastication. There was wildness in the eye of the attendant as she took the order for yet another luncheon. She fled, with the assurance that it would be ready immediately, yet subsequent events suggested that even while she spoke the sheep that was to respond to that thirty-fifth order for mutton chops was browsing in the pastures of Bandon.

For eyes that had last looked on food at 7 A.M., neither the view of the street obtainable from the first floor parlour window, nor even the contemplation of the remarkable sacred pictures that adorned its walls, had the interest they might have held earlier in the day, and the dirty cruet-stand on the dirtier tablecloth was endued with an almost hypnotic fascination in its suggestion of coming sustenance. At the end of the first hour a stupor verging on indifference had set in; it was far on in the second when the dish of fried mutton chops, the hard potatoes, and the tepid whiskies and sodas were flung upon the board. No preliminary to a week's indigestion had been neglected, and a deserved success was the result.

The business of the fair was still transacted at large throughout the hotel. From behind the mound of mutton chops a buyer shoved a roll of dirty one-pound notes round the potato dish, and after due haggling received back one, according to the mystic Irish custom of "luck-penny". On the sofa two farmers carried on a transaction in which the swap of a colt, boot money, and luck-penny were blended into one trackless maze of astuteness and arithmetic. On the wall above them a print in which Ananias and Sapphira were the central figures gave a simple and suitable finish to the scene.

The Codes Of Hammurabi And Moses
W. W. Davies

QTY

The discovery of the Hammurabi Code is one of the greatest achievements of archaeology, and is of paramount interest, not only to the student of the Bible, but also to all those interested in ancient history...

Religion   ISBN: *1-59462-338-4*   **Pages:132**
MSRP $12.95

The Theory of Moral Sentiments
Adam Smith

QTY

This work from 1749. contains original theories of conscience amd moral judgment and it is the foundation for systemof morals.

Philosophy ISBN: *1-59462-777-0*   **Pages:536**
MSRP $19.95

Jessica's First Prayer
Hesba Stretton

QTY

In a screened and secluded corner of one of the many railway-bridges which span the streets of London there could be seen a few years ago, from five o'clock every morning until half past eight, a tidily set-out coffee-stall, consisting of a trestle and board, upon which stood two large tin cans, with a small fire of charcoal burning under each so as to keep the coffee boiling during the early hours of the morning when the work-people were thronging into the city on their way to their daily toil...

Childrens   ISBN: *1-59462-373-2*   **Pages:84**
MSRP $9.95

My Life and Work
Henry Ford

QTY

Henry Ford revolutionized the world with his implementation of mass production for the Model T automobile. Gain valuable business insight into his life and work with his own auto-biography... "We have only started on our development of our country we have not as yet, with all our talk of wonderful progress, done more than scratch the surface. The progress has been wonderful enough but..."

Biographies/   ISBN: *1-59462-198-5*   **Pages:300**
MSRP $21.95

The Art of Cross-Examination
Francis Wellman

QTY

I presume it is the experience of every author, after his first book is published upon an important subject, to be almost overwhelmed with a wealth of ideas and illustrations which could readily have been included in his book, and which to his own mind, at least, seem to make a second edition inevitable. Such certainly was the case with me; and when the first edition had reached its sixth impression in five months, I rejoiced to learn that it seemed to my publishers that the book had met with a sufficiently favorable reception to justify a second and considerably enlarged edition. ..

Reference   **ISBN: *1-59462-647-2***

Pages:412

MSRP $19.95

On the Duty of Civil Disobedience
Henry David Thoreau

QTY

Thoreau wrote his famous essay, On the Duty of Civil Disobedience, as a protest against an unjust but popular war and the immoral but popular institution of slave-owning. He did more than write—he declined to pay his taxes, and was hauled off to gaol in consequence. Who can say how much this refusal of his hastened the end of the war and of slavery ?

Law   **ISBN: *1-59462-747-9***

Pages:48

MSRP $7.45

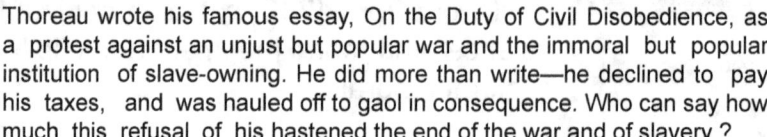

Dream Psychology Psychoanalysis for Beginners
Sigmund Freud

QTY

Sigmund Freud, born Sigismund Schlomo Freud (May 6, 1856 - September 23, 1939), was a Jewish-Austrian neurologist and psychiatrist who co-founded the psychoanalytic school of psychology. Freud is best known for his theories of the unconscious mind, especially involving the mechanism of repression; his redefinition of sexual desire as mobile and directed towards a wide variety of objects; and his therapeutic techniques, especially his understanding of transference in the therapeutic relationship and the presumed value of dreams as sources of insight into unconscious desires.

Pages:196

Psychology   **ISBN: *1-59462-905-6***

MSRP $15.45

The Miracle of Right Thought
Orison Swett Marden

QTY

Believe with all of your heart that you will do what you were made to do. When the mind has once formed the habit of holding cheerful, happy, prosperous pictures, it will not be easy to form the opposite habit. It does not matter how improbable or how far away this realization may see, or how dark the prospects may be, if we visualize them as best we can, as vividly as possible, hold tenaciously to them and vigorously struggle to attain them, they will gradually become actualized, realized in the life. But a desire, a longing without endeavor, a yearning abandoned or held indifferently will vanish without realization.

Pages:360

Self Help   **ISBN: *1-59462-644-8***

MSRP $25.45

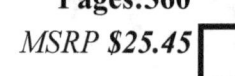

The Rosicrucian Cosmo-Conception Mystic Christianity *by Max Heindel*   ISBN: *1-59462-188-8*   **$38.95**
The Rosicrucian Cosmo-conception is not dogmatic, neither does it appeal to any other authority than the reason of the student. It is: not controversial, but is: sent forth in the, hope that it may help to clear...   New Age/Religion Pages 646

Abandonment To Divine Providence *by Jean-Pierre de Caussade*   ISBN: *1-59462-228-0*   **$25.95**
"The Rev. Jean Pierre de Caussade was one of the most remarkable spiritual writers of the Society of Jesus in France in the 18th Century. His death took place at Toulouse in 1751. His works have gone through many editions and have been republished...   Inspirational/Religion Pages 400

Mental Chemistry *by Charles Haanel*   ISBN: *1-59462-192-6*   **$23.95**
Mental Chemistry allows the change of material conditions by combining and appropriately utilizing the power of the mind. Much like applied chemistry creates something new and unique out of careful combinations of chemicals the mastery of mental chemistry...   New Age Pages 354

The Letters of Robert Browning and Elizabeth Barret Barrett 1845-1846 vol II   ISBN: *1-59462-193-4*   **$35.95**
by Robert Browning and Elizabeth Barrett   Biographies Pages 596

Gleanings In Genesis (volume I) *by Arthur W. Pink*   ISBN: *1-59462-130-6*   **$27.45**
Appropriately has Genesis been termed "the seed plot of the Bible" for in it we have, in germ form, almost all of the great doctrines which are afterwards fully developed in the books of Scripture which follow...   Religion/Inspirational Pages 420

The Master Key *by L. W. de Laurence*   ISBN: *1-59462-001-6*   **$30.95**
In no branch of human knowledge has there been a more lively increase of the spirit of research during the past few years than in the study of Psychology, Concentration and Mental Discipline. The requests for authentic lessons in Thought Control, Mental Discipline and...   New Age/Business Pages 422

The Lesser Key Of Solomon Goetia *by L. W. de Laurence*   ISBN: *1-59462-092-X*   **$9.95**
This translation of the first book of the "Lernegton" which is now for the first time made accessible to students of Talismanic Magic was done, after careful collation and edition, from numerous Ancient Manuscripts in Hebrew, Latin, and French...   New Age/Occult Pages 92

Rubaiyat Of Omar Khayyam *by Edward Fitzgerald*   ISBN: *1-59462-332-5*   **$13.95**
Edward Fitzgerald, whom the world has already learned, in spite of his own efforts to remain within the shadow of anonymity, to look upon as one of the rarest poets of the century, was born at Bredfield, in Suffolk, on the 31st of March, 1809. He was the third son of John Purcell...   Music Pages 172

Ancient Law *by Henry Maine*   ISBN: *1-59462-128-4*   **$29.95**
The chief object of the following pages is to indicate some of the earliest ideas of mankind, as they are reflected in Ancient Law, and to point out the relation of those ideas to modern thought.   Religion/History Pages 452

Far-Away Stories *by William J. Locke*   ISBN: *1-59462-129-2*   **$19.45**
"Good wine needs no bush, but a collection of mixed vintages does. And this book is just such a collection. Some of the stories I do not want to remain buried for ever in the museum files of dead magazine-numbers an author's not unpardonable vanity..."   Fiction Pages 272

Life of David Crockett *by David Crockett*   ISBN: *1-59462-250-7*   **$27.45**
"Colonel David Crockett was one of the most remarkable men of the times in which he lived. Born in humble life, but gifted with a strong will, an indomitable courage, and unremitting perseverance...   Biographies/New Age Pages 424

Lip-Reading *by Edward Nitchie*   ISBN: *1-59462-206-X*   **$25.95**
Edward B. Nitchie, founder of the New York School for the Hard of Hearing, now the Nitchie School of Lip-Reading, Inc, wrote "LIP-READING Principles and Practice". The development and perfecting of this meritorious work on lip-reading was an undertaking...   How-to Pages 400

A Handbook of Suggestive Therapeutics, Applied Hypnotism, Psychic Science   ISBN: *1-59462-214-0*   **$24.95**
by Henry Munro   Health/New Age/Health/Self-help Pages 376

A Doll's House: and Two Other Plays *by Henrik Ibsen*   ISBN: *1-59462-112-8*   **$19.95**
Henrik Ibsen created this classic when in revolutionary 1848 Rome. Introducing some striking concepts in playwriting for the realist genre, this play has been studied the world over.   Fiction/Classics/Plays 308

The Light of Asia *by sir Edwin Arnold*   ISBN: *1-59462-204-3*   **$13.95**
In this poetic masterpiece, Edwin Arnold describes the life and teachings of Buddha. The man who was to become known as Buddha to the world was born as Prince Gautama of India but he rejected the worldly riches and abandoned the reigns of power when...   Religion/History/Biographies Pages 170

The Complete Works of Guy de Maupassant *by Guy de Maupassant*   ISBN: *1-59462-157-8*   **$16.95**
"For days and days, nights and nights, I had dreamed of that first kiss which was to consecrate our engagement, and I knew not on what spot I should put my lips..."   Fiction/Classics Pages 240

The Art of Cross-Examination *by Francis L. Wellman*   ISBN: *1-59462-309-0*   **$26.95**
Written by a renowned trial lawyer, Wellman imparts his experience and uses case studies to explain how to use psychology to extract desired information through questioning.   How-to/Science/Reference Pages 408

Answered or Unanswered? *by Louisa Vaughan*   ISBN: *1-59462-248-5*   **$10.95**
Miracles of Faith in China   Religion Pages 112

The Edinburgh Lectures on Mental Science (1909) *by Thomas*   ISBN: *1-59462-008-3*   **$11.95**
This book contains the substance of a course of lectures recently given by the writer in the Queen Street Hall, Edinburgh. Its purpose is to indicate the Natural Principles governing the relation between Mental Action and Material Conditions...   New Age/Psychology Pages 148

Ayesha *by H. Rider Haggard*   ISBN: *1-59462-301-5*   **$24.95**
Verily and indeed it is the unexpected that happens! Probably if there was one person upon the earth from whom the Editor of this, and of a certain previous history, did not expect to hear again...   Classics Pages 380

Ayala's Angel *by Anthony Trollope*   ISBN: *1-59462-352-X*   **$29.95**
The two girls were both pretty, but Lucy who was twenty-one who supposed to be simple and comparatively unattractive, whereas Ayala was credited, as her Bombwhat romantic name might show, with poetic charm and a taste for romance. Ayala when her father died was nineteen...   Fiction Pages 484

The American Commonwealth *by James Bryce*   ISBN: *1-59462-286-8*   **$34.45**
An interpretation of American democratic political theory. It examines political mechanics and society from the perspective of Scotsman James Bryce   Politics Pages 572

Stories of the Pilgrims *by Margaret P. Pumphrey*   ISBN: *1-59462-116-0*   **$17.95**
This book explores pilgrims religious oppression in England as well as their escape to Holland and eventual crossing to America on the Mayflower, and their early days in New England...   History Pages 268

www.bookjungle.com *email: sales@bookjungle.com fax: 630-214-0564 mail: Book Jungle PO Box 2226 Champaign, IL 61825*

QTY

The Fasting Cure *by Sinclair Upton*   ISBN: *1-59462-222-1* **$13.95**
In the Cosmopolitan Magazine for May, 1910, and in the Contemporary Review (London) for April, 1910, I published an article dealing with my experiences in fasting. I have written a great many magazine articles, but never one which attracted so much attention... New Age/Self Help/Health Pages 164

Hebrew Astrology *by Sepharial*   ISBN: *1-59462-308-2* **$13.45**
In these days of advanced thinking it is a matter of common observation that we have left many of the old landmarks behind and that we are now pressing forward to greater heights and to a wider horizon than that which represented the mind-content of our progenitors... Astrology Pages 144

Thought Vibration or The Law of Attraction in the Thought World   ISBN: *1-59462-127-6* **$12.95**

by William Walker Atkinson   *Psychology/Religion Pages 144*

Optimism *by Helen Keller*   ISBN: *1-59462-108-X* **$15.95**
Helen Keller was blind, deaf, and mute since 19 months old, yet famously learned how to overcome these handicaps, communicate with the world, and spread her lectures promoting optimism. An inspiring read for everyone... Biographies/Inspirational Pages 84

Sara Crewe *by Frances Burnett*   ISBN: *1-59462-360-0* **$9.45**
In the first place, Miss Minchin lived in London. Her home was a large, dull, tall one, in a large, dull square, where all the houses were alike, and all the sparrows were alike, and where all the door-knockers made the same heavy sound... Childrens/Classic Pages 88

The Autobiography of Benjamin Franklin *by Benjamin Franklin*   ISBN: *1-59462-135-7* **$24.95**
The Autobiography of Benjamin Franklin has probably been more extensively read than any other American historical work, and no other book of its kind has had such ups and downs of fortune. Franklin lived for many years in England, where he was agent... Biographies/History Pages 332

Name	
Email	
Telephone	
Address	
City, State ZIP	

☐ **Credit Card**   ☐ **Check / Money Order**

Credit Card Number	
Expiration Date	
Signature	

Please Mail to: Book Jungle
PO Box 2226
Champaign, IL 61825
or Fax to: 630-214-0564

ORDERING INFORMATION
web: *www.bookjungle.com*
email: *sales@bookjungle.com*
fax: *630-214-0564*
mail: *Book Jungle PO Box 2226 Champaign, IL 61825*
or PayPal *to sales@bookjungle.com*

Please contact us for bulk discounts

DIRECT-ORDER TERMS

20% Discount if You Order Two or More Books
Free Domestic Shipping!
Accepted: Master Card, Visa, Discover, American Express

www.ingramcontent.com/pod-product-compliance
Lightning Source LLC
Chambersburg PA
CBHW080823020726

47501CB00009B/2399